Revolutions

by

Ray Leigh

Cover design by Castenzio Cusumano
Cusumano Designs Ltd

Interior design by BAD PRESS iNK

ISBN: 978-1-0687203-4-5

published by www.badpress.ink

Dedicated to JRM

REVOLUTIONS 1

Around the city like a halo of green the suburbs lie. Their inhabitants living quiet lives undisturbed by the grim grey of the density at their core. Here are the gardens and hedgerows of the comfortable. The soft lawns and tidiness of people living by their books.

From the air the orderliness is clear. The patchwork spreads in a series of squares. Each square attached to a strip of road. Some squares are larger than others and some are greener. The interiors are as ordered as the exteriors. Every ten years or so such places are rocked by the horror of domestic murder or random violent death.

Years are clocked up in service and the rewards are slowly reaped. Provision is made for the family and for the day of retirement. The road is long and hard but the rules are clear.

Within the endless blocks of squares there operates the vertical ladder of progression. Houses come terraced, semi-detached or detached. There is a price for everything and everyone. Every patchwork of squares has its lush green acres and its drier hard corners.

Look inside the doctor's house and see the cars on the drive. All around the plot the hedge grows high. The garden is mature and luxuriant. There are shrubs and roses and lawns front and back. The stone terrace is edged by low conifers and there is a path down to the pool.

Dr Jones sits there at a wrought iron table drinking vodka and tonic on summer Saturday afternoons. He has an ice bucket and a tray with the lemon, tonic, and vodka. His shorts and shirt display a good lunch corpulence, his body has much grey hair. This man's face is bloated but he was once strong. He drinks before lunch and has wine with his food and his Saturday will complete with a drink in the afternoon.

Somewhere down the road there is a drone of a lawn mower. A blackbird sings in the apple tree. He can hear Gwen clearing the table and washing up. It's humid and hot with the summer breeze that just rustles the leaves.

Beyond the pool the lawn runs to a small summer-house at the end of the garden. All around the hedge runs ten feet high. Dr Jones is breathing heavily as he clenches and unclenches his fist. He stops and pours himself some vodka. He adds tonic and clumsily a slice of the precut lemon. His dark eyes are small in the flesh of his face as he surveys his patch of the suburb. Truly he likes the pool.

A car whooshes by on the road outside. Three doors down they are playing tennis and over the back some children play somewhere. Dr Jones goes down to the pool. His belly has burst out of his shirt and over the top of his shorts. He carries his glass and scrapes his flip-flops on the path. The booze lies heavy on his brain and heavy on his body. There is a pole eight feet long with a net at its end for catching leaves out of the pool. He struggles with it for five minutes and then returns sweating to his chair at the table. Gwen sees him nervously from the window of the kitchen. She's glad the children are all out as there is distress in the air. Clouds cross the sun and it cools for a moment. She takes down the powder and begins to clean the oven.

Dr Jones lumbers to the kitchen window and looks at his wife on her knees with her head in the oven. Gwen looks up. She has plastic gloves on and is holding wire wool in her hand. Dr Jones looks at her and sneers. Gwen stands up. He leers at her. His eyes drop from her breasts and her waist to her legs. He looks back at her face. Gwen is shy and flustered. She feels humiliation but cannot account for it.

He mutters. The words slurring quietly off his wet lips: 'Gone to seed.'

Gwen doesn't hear him as he turns away from the window back to his chair at the table on the terrace.

When the oven is clean Gwen goes to the fr dge and takes out a bottle of red wine. She takes a glass from the draining board and fills it. Sitting on a kitchen stoo she can see him sitting in his chair and she drinks. Taking a towel she dries the cutlery and puts it away in the drawer with the compartments. Then she refills her glass and sits on the stool.

The bees and hoverflies work on the sunflowers that grow beside the summerhouse. Butterflies are feeding on the honeysuckle up the side of the garage. The pool is electric blue under the sun and Gwen opens another bottle of wine. Dr Jones sweats as he dozes on the hard garden chair.

Yolanda their older daughter is twelve and has been to visit her friend. Her father said be back at four-th rty and by then she has parked her bike next to his car and been in to see her mother. The house is cold and there is a wine bottle on the table. Gwen is still sitting on the stool.

Yolanda is happy and excited. This child gives out energy and light. There is a joy here that regards all as marvellous and wonderful. Enthusiasm lives in this child's bones and the excitement is constant.

'Jacky's got a pony. And I rode it. It was really good. And I can go tomorrow to help groom it and we've got to muck out and do the saddle and bridle.'

Gwen looked at her daughter. Her lipstick is a little smudged and her gums slightly stained purple. Looking at the child makes her a little giddy on the stool. There is something about this girl of hers that always disgusts her. Now she's going all horsey and stupid. How was it that her own daughter could never sit quietly and be content. Any little thing gets the child all high and excited. It was unnatural to Gwen. The child was far too full of herself and too busy with things. A girl should be quiet. She looked at Yolanda's bright eyes and red cheeks. The child's whole body was animated and alive. Her arms flapped and she moved from foot to foot as she spoke.

Gwen stared at her until the child stood quite still. She looked at her with hard eyes. Her gaze travelled up and down her daughter and could not hide its dislike. She looked in Yolanda's eyes and almost smiled as she said, 'Ask your father.'

The child bit her lip and turned around. Although her mother had stilled Yolanda her gait was defiant and all her love of life flapped in her left arm as she almost beat her chest.

Gwen slid unsteadily from her stool and rinsed out her wine glass. Through the kitchen window she could see Dr Jones slumped in his chair. She could watch as her daughter approached him.

These suburban squares bleed from their cul-de-sacs and avenues onto main roads which link onto trunk roads and carry seamless traffic to the city. At night car lights vibrate in the dark. From the orange glow of light you can feel the city more than fifty miles away. It is many miles across and all the roads lead there.

Its suburbs are green and then more dense and grey. The core is flashing lights and around its core buzzes all the grey you can see. Its people scurry chased by poverty. Fantasy and content don't find easy ground and flowers hardly grow. There are no hedges here just dividing walls and there is hardly any order in the chaos.

Here are the acres of density housing. Buy land and build the units. They would release the figures of the number of homes built. Stacked and pushed together and all within guidelines on minimum room size. They know how many square feet exactly you need to breathe.

This is the engine that drives the city day and night. The market is open and you can be bought and can be sold. This is total availability and twenty-four-hour shopping. You can toil and you can fly. It gets dark but night never falls.

113K Keats House, Ebbheath Estate. Another number in the shadow of the high rise. They don't put children above the tenth floor but they can't make order from disorder.

Sue's door is at the level of the street. It opens onto a wide passageway running between blocks of maisonettes. You can park a car here. The proper numbered spaces are round the back. Children play in groups and there is a square of grass with one rubber tyre swing.

Traffic hums past on the main road at the edge of the estate. A plane passes overhead and a baby is crying. You can hear TV and music playing. Rubbish swirls in the wind by the large bins.

The children are upstairs and are both asleep. They have new bunk beds with matching cartoon bedspreads. There are dolls on the windowsill and toys in a box. The carpet and curtains are clean and new.

Sue sits at the dining room table with matching chairs. On the table in front of her is a dye-your-own-hair kit. She is reading the instructions wearing a bathrobe and a towel on her head. The TV is on in the lounge and the radio plays in the kitchen. The washing up is done and the floors are swept.

Sue gets up and fills the kettle. She collects the instruments and gets down a mixing bowl. From the kitchen window she looks out onto the passageway and the maisonettes opposite. There are the sounds of a motorbike being revved and adolescent male laughter. The house feels empty with just her and the girls.

Will had never been away before. He had worked late and worked nights. There had been times when he only came home to sleep a few hours. When he walked out the door he worked and when he came in he brought money.

Sue had chosen new carpets and furniture this year. There had been prams for the babies and expensive toys at birthdays and Christmases. They had a big screen TV and a new washing machine. Sue bought herself something new when she wanted to go out.

He was not coming back for three weeks. This was night one. When he came back he would have enough money to take her to Spain. Laying floors with his brother in The Hague, he would really earn and Sue knew he knew what he was doing. Yet now she felt restless and bored. Too unsettled to settle and get on with her hair.

She sat in front of the TV until late and didn't sleep in her bed until dawn. Sounds in the night disturb her until she has the radio on loud. Then she turns it off and listens to the city.

Police sirens and buses through the night. Cars pulling up and the slamming of doors. Voices and laughter and cats fighting. Footsteps below her window and water in the pipes.

At four Sue makes herself some tea and smokes two cigarettes. She looks out of the kitchen window and checks what is on the TV. When she lay back in bed she thought of a dream holiday with Will and the girls. He seemed stupid and dull with his careful ways. She remembered his smell and his breath and she felt cheated and poor. Will grunted when he took off his trousers and let out little groans if he bent down.

Her restlessness was a rage against Will. She did everything right. Look at the house. Look at the girls. Sue had made this. Will was boring. He was stuck in his ways. He was not really attentive or bright or strong.

Sue lay on her front. One hand above her head and one hand between her thighs. The breath of Will was in her hair.

John was a confusion of pain. There was so much it was self-cancelling. Each breath rasped. The pressure on his chest increased. It was a weight with the highest density. Both an inch and a yard wide. He breathed and breathed and it would not ease. The skin on his bones waxed thin sweat. He breathed. Downstairs he heard a key in the latch. John called. It was the last of his strength.

He spun into a void.

Dead on arrival.

His room was a room in a house. Multiple occupancy house with rooms to let. It was twenty feet by fifteen. A double bed, a sink and old electric cooker. There was a path from the door to the bed through newspapers and empty bottles and tins of beer. Beside the bed was an ashtray and an empty bottle of sherry. The curtains were shut and the TV was off. Clothes lay in a pile.

The toilet was outside on the landing just by the door. A bathroom on the floor below. The room did not stink. John made it to the toilet. His trousers carried stains at the top of his thigh but he remained continent mostly. This was a place where a man just slept. A place to collapse. Life was somewhere else.

Of the millions of lives in the city the end of this one caused few stirs. A tired ambulance crew and a fatigued hospital staff couldn't quite tell why he had died.

Yolanda reached her father's side with an almost bold, 'Dad.'

Dr Jones never considered himself drunk. He might close his eyes but he always denied sleeping. Gwen and the children knew he was approachable when asleep drunk as he would instantly wake himself up and pay attention. He never forgot anything ever.

He had a brain that could assimilate information and retain it nearly indefinitely. It was an ability that allowed him to fly in school. Fact and detail were stored and were instantly accessible. He prioritised his data. His system never crashed.

The family life file was comprehensive and all embracing. Dr Jones conscientiously made a mental note of each movement of Gwen and the children. He could relate each movement to a progression he anticipated. Clinic appointments and school activities were logged as were most words spoken.

His few drinks by the pool on summer afternoons was on his timetable. Everything else could run on autopilot. His drinking was an internal experience. He added to his toxicity level with calculation and determination. Every week Dr Jones experimented with dosages and monitored the results. He teetered on the edge and slid sideways into unconsciousness.

Dr Jones put out his hand for Yolanda's. She had left at one o'clock having agreed with her mother to take her lunch early. Jacky her friend was the daughter of the Elstrops who lived at the top of the avenue. Mr Elstrop was a senior partner in accountancy. There were two teenage sons at public school who Dr Jones considered perhaps irresponsible but they were a good family. Mrs Elstrop was the daughter of someone and had money.

Dr Jones held his daughter's hand but kept ooking down at the garden. Yolanda stood close at her father's side. That was where he wanted her.

'Did you have a good time?'

This was polite conversation and Yolanda knew its rules.

'Yes thanks, it was really good.'

That was enough. It was not appropriate to go on any

more. Her earlier experience with her mother had been an attempt to share her joy. With her father she would not make an attempt. Meetings with Dr Jones were business-like and his children would leave with agreed action points. He was friendly and passed comment and sometimes a joke but his children lived with his obligations. Yolanda's father dropped her hand and patted her back.

'And what did you do.'

Yolanda began to report back. She stuck to the facts and offered the technical information she had gathered. A martingale she explained was attached from the girth to the reins to stop a pony from throwing its head. Yolanda detached herself from this as much as she could so as to prevent her excitement from showing. Dr Jones as much as Gwen disliked children who were too full of themselves.

Yolanda's left leg began to fidget. The tension of hold-ing down her own energy and the anxiety of asking her father for permission to go back to Jacky's tomorrow began to emerge in the flexing of her knee.

Dr Jones caught her knee gently in his hand from behind. 'Have you finished all your homework?'

Yolanda was relieved at first by her father's enquiry. She still had time to ask about her visit tomorrow. But homework was never all done. Dr Jones sensed her unease. Medical students did not know the answer to his follow up question. He knew before he asked whether they had the knowledge or not.

Dr Jones stroked the back of his daughter's leg. Yolanda breathed hard against her tension. Her mind filled with possible answers. Yes – but then he would want to see it and there would be something not right.

'Just about.'

It sounded lame and an admission of guilt. This was failure. Yolanda breathed more easily now. It had all seemed so brilliant and easy there had to be a problem. Her father gently stroked the back of her leg Now she knew the answer before she asked.

'Can I go again tomorrow?'

Dr Jones stroked his daughter.

'I don't think so.'

There was no release from Yolanda. That had come moments before. She was already disappointment and failure. The force of life she had brought back from the horse no longer flapped in her. They had taken it from her.

Sue woke up when Sharon got on top of her and said, 'Mummy wake up.'

She instantly threw her eyes at the clock radio and groaned out of bed. Sharon chattered.

'I made Emma crispies but she split the milk and now it's on the floor.'

Sue was improvising a schedule as she went into the bathroom.

'Go and get dressed and help Emma. Quickly. You'll be late for school.'

It was eight twenty-eight. Give them some toast and out the door by eight-fifty and they would only be a few minutes late for school. Emma was crying. Sue picked her up and gave her a kiss.

'Go and get dressed with Sharon. Be a good girl for Mummy. You don't want to be late.'

The toast was done. Sharon brought Emma down-stairs in school clothes. She brushed the girls' hair and tied it up with ribbons. She took a flannel from the sink and gave their faces a wipe. They left the house with Sharon and Emma carrying a piece of toast in each hand.

At school the playground was empty. The children were already in class. Sue told Sharon to go to class. She took Emma herself and opened the classroom door. Miss Crawford looked up and Sue caught her eye and smiled while drawing Emma into the room. She left her child on the threshold and closed the door.

The clock in the foyer said ten past nine. Sue felt funnily elated. The kids were at school; she had until three-thirty all to herself. She felt the back pocket of her jeans. Bingo – one cigarette, the last of the packet.

As she smoked Sue found herself dawdling home. Will would not be home tonight so there were only the kids to think about. The rest of her life was hers.

Dr Jones watched Yolanda in the pool swimming lengths. He was sipping his last drink to sober himself up. It was five-fifteen and dinner would be at six.

June Smith was the daughter of the vicar and a sensible girl. The Smiths were officially family friends. Dr Jones filed June as prudent and responsible. She was a student who looked studious and dressed sensibly and did not attract men. Dr Jones would always give her some money for taking the little ones out. He knew how tight financial matters were on a grant. Gwen would take back the children and say, 'June you must say hello to Richard.'

June came out onto the patio. Dr Jones got up saying 'Hello,' arranged another chair and offered the young woman a drink. June refused but was flattered by her inclusion in the adult world of alcohol. She sat almost opposite the doctor but not quite. He could still watch Yolanda as she swam in the pool.

'How're things at university?'

June talked about her second-year exams and her thesis in her third year. She was wearing a blouse and a knee-length skirt. Her body was large and not quite flabby with heavy bones. Her large feet were in flat sandals and she wore steel-rimmed glasses. She had a fringe but her hair was also tied back. The blouse buttoned up to where the collarbones met. It was made of light white manmade fabric and hung tight over her breasts. There was a gap where it opened an inch through which you could see her bra. The skirt was a floral print.

'And what of your fellow students.'

June Smith laughed and began to tell of the various types. Dr Jones watched Yolanda and glanced at June Smith's eyes. Her eyes followed his and she too watched Yolanda swim.

She mentioned a few of her friends and spoke of some things they did together. Dr Jones looked at her breasts and June Smith watched Yolanda. When June Smith glanced at Dr Jones he would stare at the pool.

He shifted on his chair and took a small sip of h s drink. June crossed her legs with her left hand in her lap.

'How do you find the teaching staff?'

June laughed and put her hands behind her head. Her breasts strained against her blouse. Dr Jones could see the imprint of the pattern of her bra against the white material. He could see the brown of her nipples.

June put down her arms and watching the pool told of the strange ways of some of her lecturers. She strained her spine a little and swung her leg gently from below the knee. Her hand was between her thighs.

Dr Jones looked at her breasts. Her nipples seemed prominent. He looked at her face. She seemed hot. June Smith stopped talking. Dr Jones said nothing. She sat there watching his daughter swimming and he sat there staring at her breasts. Her leg swung gently. June Smith sighed.

Dr Jones almost echoed it and commented, 'It's hot, are you sure about that drink.'

'No, I'm fine.'

They sat on in silence. Dr Jones slumped a little in his chair. His left hand held his drink against his right thigh and his forearm lay on his groin.

Yolanda had stopped swimming and was lying on a lilo. June Smith ran her right hand through her hair. As she raised it her right breast moved against her blouse. The breast changed shape and stood proud. Dr Jones stared at it watching its nipple. June Smith closed her eyes as her hand played with her hair. Her breast strained hard against her bra and her bra strained hard against her blouse. Her mouth was slightly open. Dr Jones broke in to a sweat on his forehead. Gwen shouted from the kitchen.

'Richard, ask June if she's staying for tea.'

Dr Jones looked at the pool. June Smith opened her eyes and looked at the pool.

'Gwen wants to know if you'll stay for tea.'

'No thanks, I must get back.'

Dr Jones followed her to the house. Her calves were heavy and she had no visible ankles. Yolanda ran past them to get changed. He staggered a bit from the drink.

Inside the house Dr Jones went to his jacket and took twenty pounds from his wallet. He waited by the front door. June said goodbye to the children and Gwen. He offered June the money and she politely refused. Then he encouraged her suggesting she might find it useful for a textbook next term. June acquiesced and left.

The heat of the afternoon had broken. Yolanda came downstairs ready for tea. Adrian and Miranda were already at the table. Dr Jones went and joined them. His afternoon drink by the pool was over. He planned to take part in happy family life until eight. After that he would watch TV and finish the vodka. He entered the dining room and the children went quiet.

After tea Yolanda loaded the dishwasher with her mother. Yolanda did most of it while her mother watched, waiting for her to make a slip. Gwen washed two saucepans in the sink and set the dishwasher. Afterwards she looked around the kitchen. Yolanda looked too and anticipating her mother picked up the salt and pepper and put them in the cupboard. Gwen sat on the stool with a vague grimace.

'Go and watch TV.'

Sue picked up the phone and then replaced it. It was just after noon. The girls came out of school at three-thirty. Will would be back in three weeks. There was nothing for her to do that could not wait until tomorrow or a week's time. She sat down in a torpor of aimlessness.

The radio was on. It was the hottest day in the city this year and the forecast was good. A great day for sunbathing. Eighty-five degrees. The next tune was the girl's favourite *I could be so happy.* The song reached Sue and Sue got to her feet. She faced a mood change. As she smiled, she almost danced and thought of how good it was to have some time without Will. She turned the radio up in the kitchen and went upstairs.

I could be so happy, happy, happy, happy… the tune ended. Sue repeated the last line and thought if only he was never coming back. The thought amused her and she kept it. Sue went into the girls' room and tidied up the few stray toys and clothes. In her room she straightened the duvet and the makeup on her dressing table.

Out the window she looked down into her back yard.

The radio was louder now. Sue locked into the restless good time patter of the DJ. It was a beautiful day for everyone out there to have a good time. Jingles and station identification and now for the latest from the news room at twelve-thirty. A man's voice with a professional sense of excitement.

Sue rolled onto her back and tried to get comfortable. She was having a good time sunbathing.

This was the advantage of Will going away. She could relax without thinking about when he would come back from work. If the weather stayed good, she would soon have a tan.

Sue got up and went into the house and brought out two cushions from the settee. She arranged them and lay down. The radio played a soul tune. Sue tried to release the restlessness that had been with her all last night and this morning. She tried to settle her mind and ease her body. She ran through the day's routine and the chores for the week. Nothing was pressing. Everything could wait. She got up and went into the house.

Sue made herself a cup of tea and went upstairs to get her sunglasses. She picked up the magazine from the front room and another cushion for her head.

Back in the yard she made herself comfortable lying on her front reading the magazine drinking tea. Then she got up and went to pick up her cigarettes, matches, and an ashtray. Lying back down she exhaled. Now she had everything. She exhaled a sigh again.

The paved back yard was a twelve-foot square. It had a board wood fence about six feet high all around with a gate. Yards were used for drying washing and storing bits of furniture. A few had plants in pots. Some had dogs. The police helicopter circled over the high street and then bore away. The refuse men were chattering and abusing their way along the road at the back. A car engine revved and screamed and then cut out. The sun glared through the dirt haze of the city. There was no wind.

'This one's for the ravers,' and the radio gave out a burst of manic computer riffs. A siren began to get closer and then began to fade. Sue got up and went inside and up to her bedroom. She looked at herself in the dressing room mirror. Her shorts were creased and worn. Her vest top looked dull and unfresh. She tied back her hair and looked through her clothes. She found another pair of shorts and a bikini top.

The yard was a sun trap. Sue flexed in the heat. She closed her eyes and snuggled her head into the crook of her arm. The sun pricked at her skin. She wriggled her toes. She tried to relieve the tension. The almost sleepless night had left her body tired but her mind would not close down. She fidgeted a little on the cushions looking for sleep. There was anxiety about the night ahead. Would it be the long wait for dawn of the night before.

Sue breathed and looked down at her leg. She flexed her calf muscle and then her thigh. She tensed and released her backside. Her head swung round and she looked over the other shoulder at her other leg. Sue tensed and relaxed it and let her head drop back into her arm. A breeze fluttered the page of her magazine.

A moment later she turned on her back and lit a cigarette. She picked up the magazine and could find nothing of interest. She smoked and looked at the back of her house. Idly Sue counted the number of paving stones in the yard.

She put out the cigarette and lay back on her front. She could feel her skin warming and hotting. Her body temperature increased until her cheek sweated where it rested on her arm. Slowly her skin began to burn.

Someone dropped a saucepan and someone bellowed 'Don.' A window opened and a car started up. A doorbell rang and an aeroplane passed. Sue still chased sleep and fidgeted occasionally. She thought how long twenty nights without sleep could be.

With the window open Alan could see Sue without pressing his face against the glass. His upstairs bedroom just overlooked her back yard. To see over the fence, he would have to stand on a chair. He stuck three cigarette papers together and broke up a cigarette. He burnt the hash with a disposable lighter and rolled up the reefer. He stood on the chair and drew on the joint. The first wave crept over his brain. He got down and sat on his bed drawing heavily again and waiting.

Miranda and Adrian lay on the floor watching the TV. Yolanda sat in an armchair. Dr Jones opened the door, looked at his children and closed it again. He went into the kitchen. Gwen was sitting on her stool with a glass of wine in her hand. Dr Jones looked directly into her face. She looked down at the floor. He took a glass from the cupboard and ice and tonic from the fridge. The vodka bottle was next to the kettle.

With his drink in his hand, he lent back on the kitchen door and drank from his glass. He looked at this wife and spoke.

'You're drunk.'

Gwen still looked at the floor and raised her glass to her lips. She was cowed.

Dr Jones took another drink from his glass. One of Gwen's heels slipped off the bar of the stool. She replaced it. Her glass was held by both hands in her lap. Her head was down.

Dr Jones put down his glass. He took two steps across the room and hissed as he drove his right fist into his wife's ribs. Gwen crashed off of the stool onto the floor with her head against the door of the cupboard where the shoe cleaning stuff was kept.

'You're very drunk,' said Dr Jones, from where he stood above her.

Gwen did not cry out because of the children. Dr Jones went to watch TV.

John lay in cubicle seven. A hurried nurse spoke. 'There's an unknown deceased in seven and...' which was only part of the sentence.

An eighteen-year-old student nurse was told to wash him and lay him out. She felt weak and faint. Her hands shook.

Staff Nurse Lucerne put her head around the door. She looked at the student nurse. 'I'll get you a morgue sheet,' she said. The student nurse was left with the grim death and her tasks. She wore gloves. His clothes were in a plastic *Patients' property*. Removing his trousers had been an intimate struggle.

Staff Nurse Lucerne returned and put the morgue sheet down. She looked at the student.

'You can cut off his underwear,' which was sympathy and understanding.

Dead is inanimate and flesh is heavy. This young woman sweated fresh young sweat as she washed him. John's face glowed clean under the efficient soap. She even did between his toes. Her thoroughness was a discipline to calm her quaking. She tried to turn him so she could stuff his rectum. She couldn't even raise his shoulder. When she held his arm, she saw his hand move. Nausea oiled in her mouth.

She looked in his face. He looked back. She went outside. Her gloves dripped. She took them off. There was a mirror. The young woman looked at her face. She was still there. She tried a smile.

'Have you finished?'

'No, I can't turn him.'

Staff Nurse Lucerne went into the cubicle and the student followed. Staff Nurse Lucerne put on gloves and the student put on gloves.

Staff Nurse Lucerne leant across John's body, her breasts touched his chest. Her arm went deep under his back. Her live warmth met his soft cooling. The student looked on. Staff Nurse Lucerne put him onto his side. They rearranged his arms and legs and then John flopped onto his front. This was knowing death.

Staff Nurse Lucerne rested her hand on the back of John's neck. Her face was easy and her arm was limp.

'There's nothing to be afraid of,' she said, and left.

Alan turned on the music and lit another joint. The bass boomed and the sequencers repeated high riffs. He shuddered and shuffled from foot to foot. He pulled with his lips on the loose mixture of hash and tobacco and sighed. He rocked his spine.

Alan felt his testicles in the palm of his hand. He checked his face in the mirror. The red veins in his eyes pleased him. He smoked and blew smoke rings. With the last of the reefer in his hand he stood on the chair.

He was high and his system was charged. He stared at Sue and felt the full-on psychosis. His heart beat was up and the music filled the space behind him.

'Yeah, rockin,' he murmured.

The end of the joint burnt his finger. Alan got down and outed it in the ashtray. He circled his small room. The bass shuddered and Alan shuddered. He was there now. There.

The sun shone and Sue finally fell into the lightest of doses. Just semi-conscious as her eyes stayed shut. Hearing the cars and the buses but not starting or fidgeting. Her hair was just wet at the roots of her fringe as she sweated. A butterfly blew over the yard.

Alan fondled his hash. It was a solid half ounce block.

He sat on his bed and tossed it from hand to hand. Deliberately he began the process of rolling a third joint. After he had stuck the papers together he changed the tune. After he had broken the cigarette he adjusted the tone controls. Before he burnt the hash he walked over to the window. He sat back down and finished the job.

Sue snapped out of her thirty-second doze with saliva running out of her mouth. She raised her head two inches and lay it back on her arm. Her eyes closed again but sleep evaded her. She could hear a bass booming overlaid with high random electronic squiggles. It gently woofed in her ears.

Alan was back on his chair staring at Sue. He gazed at her back. His lips moved and he muttered, 'beautiful.'

His left hand was inside his loose trousers adjusting his prick. In his right hand he held the joint. Alan's heartbeat was up and blood rang in his ears.

Sue's arm had gone numb. She lifted her head stiffly and lay on her side. Gently she turned on her back and propped herself on her elbows. Sue took in her surroundings as if she had been away and eased herself down flat. Her arm lay across her face shielding her eyes from the sun.

Alan watched her and his heart thumped. He stood on the chair frozen still in case a movement betrayed him. He fought the pressure in his veins by half closing his eyes and exhaling through his teeth.

Something gripped his brain.

'I'll have you,' he muttered again and again.

Sue could see a puff of cloud crossing the sky through a spyhole formed by the bend of her arm resting on her nose. Now the heat from the sun warmed her throat and she closed her eyes. She opened them and watched another cloud through the spyhole. Somehow she felt disturbed and suddenly she sat up and reached for her cigarettes.

Alan swayed back as Sue sat up and hung for a moment before heavily stepping off the chair. She held the match alight as his foot thudded to the floor and she half-hesitated sensing the movement. She glanced around before moving back. Her arm recreated her spyhole.

Alan giggled a little and then cautiously stood back on the chair. Reassured that Sue was still there he got back down and put the music on maximum volume. He circled his room three times jerking his head with the beat.

Sue felt the increasing volume, she half raised her head and saw Alan's window was open and realised its source. Sue laid back down easily. There was no threat.

Alan stood on the chair and watched Sue. He concentrated his eyes on her thighs and breasts. Sometimes he looked into her face. Sue kept her eyes closed and listened to the music over the sounds of the day.

Her head dropped to the left. Through the crook of her arm she could see Alan's head where the window was ajar. She did not flinch at all. Her body felt relaxed and her flesh warm under the heat of the sun. His head moved back and forth.

Sue drew her right hand across her soft tummy. Alan inclined his head. She rested her hand back on her side. A moment later she brushed her thigh as though a fly had landed. His head moved forward. She let go a breath and raised her arm above her head. Her breast moved in the cup of the bikini. Sue gently rocked the length of her leg on her heel. Alan leant forward an inch and gritted his teeth.

Dr Jones sat in an armchair. Miranda and Adrian sat at either end of the couch. Yolanda lay on the floor. The TV was showing a game show. None of the children had stirred when their father entered the room. Their silence and concentration was fed through fear. Dr Jones exhaled and sank into his chair. The children eased their bodies.

Outside cars passed the house. Three youths stood at the bus stop and in the early evening warmth the bustle of the day continued. Lawn mowers and garden chairs were put away across the suburb. People retreated indoors and took early baths. Women cooked for husbands and guests. It was still three hours before dark.

Dr Jones closed his eyes. Adrian glanced at him from the corner of his eye. Miranda glanced too. The fear lifted a little. Yolanda sensed the two younger children relaxing and some tension fell from her shoulders. She looked round and her father was still on his chair. As she looked back at the TV there was a half-smile on her lips. Adrian suppressed a giggle and Miranda fidgeted.

The road past the house of the Jones's ran direct into the centre of the town. Now the shops were closing except for the alcohol merchants. Cars drew up outside and people emerged with tinkling bottles. Here there was no sign of poverty or need.

Gwen tied up the sack of rubbish from the bin in the kitchen and put it outside in its place beside the garage. She was unsteady from the wine and shaken from the fall. There was an ache on the left side of her ribcage. For some reason she thought of her mother as she turned to go back into the kitchen. Gwen saw the garden and the pool and the garage and the drive and knew she had everything her mother had wanted her to have. There was a slight sharp pain in her side if she took a deep breath.

Dr Jones had let his head drop to one side. His breathing had become heavier. Adrian threw a small cushion at Miranda who threw it at Yolanda. Yolanda looked at her sister and gave her a grimace that was funny with a little despair before letting go of the cushion with force at her brother who ducked. The cushion bounced off the wall and rattled into a small side table. For a moment the children froze before they heard their father's next deep breath and then they all smiled and struggled to keep silent. Yolanda stood up and retrieved the cushion and lay down with it under her chin.

Dr Jones's mouth began to rattle as he began to fall into sleep. When the rattle exploded into a snore in his nose he leapt awake but kept his body still. His eyes were startled and slid around the room looking for an enemy. He adjusted his posture in his chair and surveyed his children. He focused on the TV and asked, 'Is this worth watching?' And when there was no immediate answer he continued, 'Oh, it's that funny fella is it? He can be amusing.' And then he paused, 'Yolanda, come and sit here.'

Yolanda walked to his chair and her father gently pulled her onto his lap. She put her head on his shoulder and his pudgy fingers gently scratched her scalp. Miranda looked at her big sister and felt a creeping envy.

There was no fear in the room now. Adrian chewed on his nails and felt free to quietly spit the debris down at his feet. Gwen came in and sat on the couch between her two younger children. Miranda crept up close to her.

Dr Jones slid down in his chair a little. Yolanda could

feel his warmth all along her. He scratched her head with one hand and repositioned her legs a little with the other.

Down in the bowels of the hospital there is no decoration, just bare concrete walls. There is the service level where cooks and laundry men walk along corridors with maintenance men and joiners. Here the uniforms are industrial green and trolleys wait by lifts loaded with food or clean sheets. There are piles of black plastic rubbish sacks and pallets loaded with brown cardboard boxes. As you walk you pass doors that may be open to reveal forty people processing foul laundry or preparing steaming food. The signs read *Stores* and *Maintenance* or *Engineers* and *Medical supplies*.

The older porter was forty and wore a cravat. He had five different pens in the top pocket of his hospital shirt. The younger man followed his quick step just a pace behind. As they passed through the bustle you could see a sense of purposefulness.

The trolley was waist high and like a wheeled stretcher. Its bed was cold stainless steel and slightly concave to keep cleaning simple. At each end there was a bar handle that was yellow. It was a specialist piece of equipment.

The older porter pulled it and the younger man pushed. No one spoke to them or made any banter. The kitchen assistants and laundry men waiting in the lift knew what this trolley was for.

The older man looked round and into the eyes of his colleague. They had a shared determination in their walk and their manner. The young man was going to be OK. His eyes still held fear and he could not keep them from passing over the smudges and spots on the gently curved stainless steel.

They took the trolley down a narrow side corridor. At the end was a small lift just used for rubbish. Outside it the black bags were piled high. Inside it stank and there were squashed food scraps on the floor. In the corner was a dirty piece of dressing with a little blood. The trolley only just fit inside and the two men were pushed hard against the wall to get in. The young man rested his arms on the side of the trolley before standing up straight with a sudden realisation.

The lift slowly wound up and rocked and bounced against the side of the shaft. When the doors opened both men came out, but the younger returned and stood across the doors with his finger holding down the doors open button. The porter with the cravat looked around with the eyes of a strategist.

From the lift there was a short side corridor which led into the main corridor. The main corridor had four bays set off it. Each bay had four curtained cubicles. Number 7 was in the second bay along. No patients or members of the public were to see the trolley with or without its load.

The porter walked the length of the corridor. At its head was a large desk. No one was there. The porter turned and came back, but this time walked into each bay then returned to the lift.

The younger man's finger was still pressed on the doors button. When he relaxed it or changed fingers, the doors began to close, before being caught back as the button was depressed.

'We'll have to wait a minute. They've got something

on,' said the older man.

The younger man just nodded and changed fingers and the door jarred as if to close. All his anxiety pushed through his finger onto the button. His flesh was red around the nail, and white around his knuckle.

The porter with the cravat paced up and down the side corridor.

REVOLUTIONS 2

Later it is dark. In the suburb the traffic quietens to the occasional whoosh past the house of Dr Jones. Gwen lies sleeping on the couch. The children are upstairs in their bedrooms. The doctor drinks strong coffee.

House by house, road by road, the town darkens as the men and women retreat to bed extinguishing their lights. Some young people congregate at some quiet address, play music, and with the flux of alcohol their sexes would mix. There was not much dissonance from the ordered scheme of things here – hardly any entropy from the status quo.

Dr Jones roamed his territory. Out on the patio he bathed in the automated security light. The garage was shut. In the kitchen the work surfaces were clean. The front door was locked and the dining room table was laid for breakfast. He allowed the lounge to look lived in. He looked at his wife.

There was a time when he would have wanted her. Not now but then as a younger man he always made sure he made time for her. Gwen had always retreated before him and maybe squirmed a little but never shirked her duty of compliance. At the very beginning his heat had spread across to her and loosened her. But he always came back at her, harder and demanding and brutal, sometimes cold and specific. Dr Jones would charm her and administer increasing dosages of alcohol and charm her and as she was drunk help himself to her. For Gwen it was Richard's way. It always had been.

He sat back down in the armchair zapping the TV remote disengaged from the electronic images. Interestingly his chemical pathology as the vodka was processed out left him carrying a burden of desire. Not even late-night erotica from the box in the corner engaged this. His unconscious pliant wife presented no interest and he again stood and stalked his own premises. There was no ease of mind for this man as his bulk moved around the quiet house amongst his unconscious family.

Out there the suburb was lit by yellow dot ribbon lights and you can see how the town lies as a cluster on the land forming the north side of an estuary. In the dark the estuary waters a steel mirror between the arms of land, land holding towns made of houses in one of which a man paced burning and engorged.

Dark fell on the city. And the city geared up for night, for the economy of night, for the alignment of mutual interests that the city always offered but more so after dark.

Sue's afternoon had broken with the time check from the DJ and a dash to the school then the rigid push through of routine, of teas and baths and bed for Sharon and Emma. Then the girls slept and the house rattled empty of the presence of Will. Still sticky from the afternoon in the sun Sue bathed. Getting out she admired her own body in the long mirror Will had screwed in the wall. She looked at herself in profile and with her left hand cupped her left breast.

With a satisfied grin she pulled and twisted the nipple so it stood long. As the boys around here said she was fit.

Downstairs she had eaten and watched television drama as the sun had sunk throwing a thousand lurid pinks into the sky so densely corrupt with all the discharge from the millions of engines that throbbed across the city streets. Under her robe she wore a new set of knickers and bra.

She set the answerphone and did not pick up when calls clicked through from Lynn and Brenda. Wi fully she spurned contact from those who cared. Will would not call except on Saturday or in case of an emergency. He explained that he could not cope with hearing before he had to sleep alone in a dormitory. It was better this way.

Outside through the estate most retreated indoors but some stepped out. Those who stepped out fed the city's night hunger for labour and commodity and for the relentless seeking of gratification. Some cleaned some grafted. Some peddled drugs or flesh. Sue felt the movements of vehicles and exclamation of the dwellers with comfortable familiarity. She did not want her sister at the door now. Reaching on the sofa with a mug of warm tea and a cigarette Sue oozed her confident woman's power of attraction and enticement. From that dark root deep beyond all technology, previous to all science, she knew that the afternoon air had caused an application of tension that must stir again and move.

Staff Nurse Lucerne was ready and signalled the porters. All the cubicles were closed off with curtains and no patients could view the trolley and porters as they progressed from the lift to bay seven. Pushing through the curtain the older man led in the trolley and the younger man who looked pallid with a little sweat on his downed upper lip.

The body lay on the bed. Another nurse was just pinning shut the flap over the face that was part of the morgue sheet. It was crowded with two porters, two nurses, the trolley and the curtains billowing. Eight hands were moving the trolley alongside the bed. Staff Nurse Lucerne pumped up the bed until it was level with the trolley. The other nurse absented herself with an, 'If you're OK now.'

The senior porter moved behind the head. The younger porter stood by the feet.

'Like this,' said the elder, drawing the sheet in tight handfuls around the shoulders. The younger man followed at his station. There was eye contact and John's body was lurched, his head rocked, his arms splayed down as the two men took the strain via the sheet. They began a heft onto the trolley with a side step to transfer the weight across.

No one had applied the brake to the trolley. As John's body lurched up and across, the sagging length bowed and his arse knocked the stainless-steel vehicle away. His weight fell into the arms of the porters who both buckled and staggered a little. Collapsing in at the waist the body headed for the floor.

Lucerne nimbly got there and threw an arm under the small of John's back. With the other arm she caught hold of the trolley and applied the brake with her right foot. The porters both stood back a step and Lucerne upped the sagging waist and with a thump and a lolling of the head arms and feet John lay on the cold concave steel. There was a collective giggle.

The journey began with the porter checking the corridor was clear before wheeling out, feet first as required, John on the trolley. Lucerne gathered up the thin brown file and followed as the younger porter led the trolley to the lift.

Inside it was intimately cramped and the fear in the young man sat closely with a strong sexual attraction to Lucerne whose clear eyes and skin stood with the curve of her breasts under the blue of her uniform.

The older porter by John's head muttered his way through the Lord's prayer. His chewed fingernails gripped the handle and his face sported a poorly executed shave allowing grey stubble to establish itself in a patch on one side of his chin. His dark hair was flattened with oil in a side parting and carried miscellaneous flecks of something. Lucerne crossed her arms with the file across her chest as the younger man's eyes slid down her body. John lay on the trolley.

At basement level the doors jarred open. Here there were no public or patients and the trolley bolted out into the corridor. Now amongst their peers the porters pushed on with a certainty that their task was clearly ranked in importance above all others. Domestics and laundry men and maintenance and supplies and lab men and all, even the medical, stood aside away from their transport.

After a short run down the main corridor they swung straight through a set of fire doors into a narrower passageway barely able to accommodate the trolley and Lucerne walking alongside. They drew up broadside to a door with an intercom.

'Press it,' said the older to the younger porter.

The buzzer buzzed and the door lock clicked open and the younger man pushed and pulled the door until it opened and they manoeuvred the trolley into the narrow space before another set of double doors. There was a notice with some regulatory text regarding entering the hospital mortuary. The first set of doors completed their closure with a click and again John and his trio of companions were confined closely. The senior porter reached for another intercom and then the doors clicked open and the floor surface became tiled as they entered the morgue.

Upstairs in the house of Dr Jones away from areas that might require to be public there was a different regime. The bathroom was all clutter and the sink was unused and like the bath unclean. Towels unwashed lay over the heater and spilt out from the door of an open airing cupboard door. Used razors lay discarded on the windowsill. An economy pack of ten toilet rolls was ripped open and the top left on the cistern. Unclean clothes collected in corners and shampoo bottles collected dust and grunge on half-closed caps.

Next door was Richard and Gwen's room. There was a king-sized bed with a mass of pillows piled randomly against the headboard each with an apparently different cover. The bedding was two or three different items with a quilt and then a coverlet and even a blanket in chaos. All surfaces were covered in brushes and combs and magazines and then a stack of socks or a discarded wrapper for tights. There was a corner where Gwen's unclean underwear was visible.

Opposite the door were the windows over the front

garden and from there over the hedge you could see the road. On the wall to the left of the far side of the bed was the walk-in wardrobe where Dr Jones kept organized his shirts, underwear, suits and socks, under concealed lighting and with the inside of the doors mirrored. There was a little shelf with nail clippers and clothes brushes and a stainless-steel bar for his shoes.

Past the bathroom past their room was the spare room with a double divan, no curtains and several collections of domestic miscellaneous and cardboard boxes. The next room was small with one window and a single divan bed lying longways from the wall with the door to the wall with the window. Next to the foot of the bed was a chest of drawers under the window. There was a length of loose unfitted carpet on the small floorspace that was left. It was a room maybe eight feet by six and would have been described by estate agents as a box room. On the wall above the bed were marks from adhesive that had once held up posters.

At the end of the landing was another large room. A large piece of furniture resembling a wardrobe had been placed mid-way on the far wall to divide its space. On each side of this was a bed and a set of drawers. Immediately to the left of the door was a set of bunk beds on which lay various toys and boxes and even a pushchair.

There was one other room upstairs, which housed on a raised board the entire model train network of Dr Jones. This room was kept locked and overlooked a garden at the back of the house.

The moon sat full in a clear sky over the suburb. A fox padded across lawns and through hedges, a baby rabbit in its mouth. Bats swirled through the lanes on the edge of town and an owl patrolled where the dwellings meet with fields. Although the temperature had dropped the residual heat did not hardly dissipate and Dr Jones approached Gwen on the couch in shorts, underwear and a T-shirt.

He placed a foot on her tummy and rocked her. Increasing the motion until her head jolted on the pillow. He almost overbalanced and hopped a step away aggravated. Next he approached her with his hand in her hair and squeezed a fistful until the roots pulled at her scalp. She stirred and her eyes opened and she muttered

'I'm going,' before falling away again unconscious.

This time the doctor pushed his hands between her thighs from behind and jabbed through her skirt at her anus with his thumb. With the third shove she moved below the pressure and he shoved again his thick digit at her and broke through the alcoholic stupor.

He stepped back and she sat up momentarily resting her elbows on her knees. Then she raised herself up, walked past him, defiantly close, walked upstairs with a concentrated lightness, unclipped her bra and fell onto their bed snuggling under the heaped covers before falling again instantly asleep.

Adrian and Miranda slept on in the room with the wardrobe divider. Yolonda slept on in the smallest bare room. Downstairs Dr Jones turned off the light.

The moon pulled the water from the sea into the estuary and rising and flooding the tide surges upshore to the city. In the city the sky is squeezed away from sight by the buildings and living there you hardly glimpse the white orb in the dark sky above. Sue knew nothing of tides and

moons but somehow no surprise pulsed through her when the bell on her front door gave a brief urgent ring.

On her feet she felt the rush and tingle of expectation and caught a deep breath. Perhaps as she approached the door she thought it might not be what she expected. At the foot of the stairs there was a small round mirror and she saw herself there, her face lit by a suppressed grin and her skin still fresh with a glow from the bath.

She opened the door three inches and peered out clasping her robe shut at the collarbone. Alan stood there. He was nineteen, he wore clean jeans and a sheen of hair treatment glossed his short hair. The threshold of her house was putting Sue above him and she reviewed him, her face set in a quizzical laugh.

Alan shuffled with blatant unease, his daring gone until suddenly he met her eyes with an almost anger. He started, 'I thought I'd check on you, see if you're alright,' but faded and glanced away before finding enough to come back with, 'Anything you want?'

Sue hardly hesitated before stepping aside and opening the door and getting him inside with a backward nod of her head. He slipped past her inside. As Sue closed the door she looked out onto the passageway up and down, to see if the young man's entrance to her home had been surveyed. She looked up at the windows for a face peering out or the twist of a curtain. There was nothing she could see and maybe no one had seen him.

Alan did not move from his position three paces from the front door. She turned her hand no longer holding her robe walked past him and said, 'Come in.'

And now he was in, in the lounge looking for the next move, moving with uncertainty but knowing that a power now lay with him.

'I'm alright actually,' and Sue's voice carried a certain strain. She looked at his lean arms, a tattoo of a snarling leopard on the inside of his forearm. He stood uncomfortable unable to establish proprietorship. It was tense.

'I've got some wicked weed,' as an offering but one giving him all the ardour.

'No,' said Sue, pulling back from this path.

'No,' again, and controlling this intercourse and the trajectory offered by the narcotic. A stasis now and he clouded with disappointment but Sue lifted it with, 'The thing is I haven't got any drink.'

'I'll get some.'

'Oh great – hang on let me get it.'

A rapid spiral now and she went to the cupboard and pulled out ten pounds from the wedge that Will had left her. Alan's eyes watched her.

Within moments he was gone and within minutes he was back and Sue had left the door on the latch so when it was clear he could let himself in. And he had a glass tumbler full of vodka and so did she and he was putting together a joint of tobacco and marijuana and Sue had turned off the telly and was playing her tape and Alan was talking.

'Nah you've got to enjoy yourself, you're only young once – that's how I see it – have a good time, let yourself go, we all end up dead in the end.'

Sue looked at him. Fifteen minutes ago nothing could touch her world. Back then Sue and Emma and Sharon were safe in the hands of Will. Back then.

Now Alan had lit the joint and the vodka with a splash

of lemonade was hitting her system and she looked at him and she saw he had strong thighs and a broad neck. On his second pull on the spliff Alan leaned back in his chair in an exaggerated moment of enjoyment. He caught Sue's eye, a little lustful smirk on his lips before she felt it and turned away to the table to reach for the bottle.

Staff Nurse Lucerne and the two porters faced the refrigeration unit with its seven doors. There was more than enough room to rotate the trolley. The floor tiles gleamed under florescent lights and the doors of the fridges were matt clean. While the older porter emitted a satisfied snort at the completion of his responsibilities, the younger looked around with naked anxiety. He had not been here before.

Lucerne made her way to the glassed off office space with the brown file. On the table outside there was a large bound book. It was specified procedure that required the staff nurse to log the deceased. As she bent to her task Derek Gerrard stood up from his desk inside the office and came to watch over her shoulder. He stood unnecessarily close.

Derek Gerrard was the morgue porter contracted to spend the rest of his working life tending to the task of refrigerating the dead. There was a lot more to his role within the morgue than simply admitting and logging the deceased. There was a lot more to his position than dealing with attractive young nurses coming into his mortuary.

Lucerne had entered unknown across the spaces for name and next of kin. This deeply troubled Derek but as he could not cite an appropriate alternative procedure he let it go and did not rebuke or correct Lucerne, who uncomfortable with his closeness, hurried the task and moved away back to the trolley. Derek then entered a number of his own into the ledger.

An uneasy pause developed. Derek looked at the nurse and two porters with an amiable contempt before grudgingly giving out, 'Number four, three down.'

The older porter moved towards the door with a small white plaque with the number 4 on it. Lucerne and the young man stood in an inhibited stasis under the cold gaze of Derek Gerrard.

There was a feeling of gross incompetence being displayed beneath the eyes of an expert. The older porter had opened door four to revel five racks stacked one above the other. Some were already occupied. Hesitantly the younger porter tried to show willing by beginning to push the trolley, with John aboard, towards the open door.

Derek exhaled with impatience and contempt. These idiots had no fucking clue. His fat feet wore with some pride a pair of blue surgeon's rubber theatre shoes and they flapped as he took a couple of paces from his office. With a heavy hand he pulled from an alcove the morgue trolley. The morgue trolley superseded the deceased transport trolley with a higher level of mechanical engineering and brute functionality. Derek's heavy arm locked straight and his trolley skated over the tiled floor and clunked alongside John on his transport.

Derek waddled across the gap from the office to the fridges his porky figure garbed in full surgical greens to complement his shoes. He affected a nonchalance that threw insolence in the face of Lucerne, or anyone who failed to respect his unique position. Exhaling dramatically and throwing the young porter a split second of eye contact, Derek lent over his empty trolley and gripped John's morgue sheet at the waist and the shoulders. With a grunt and another exhalation Derek straightened his back and John's body flipped up, off its retiring place and thudded and shuddered and lolloped onto the morgue trolley.

Lucerne's set features betrayed her contempt and disgust. There was no care or respect in this operation and her pride was hurt. Derek enjoyed that. He bent and cranked the morgue trolley so that John rose to shoulder height. Now it would be easy to unclip the tray and roll him into the fridge.

'Alright,' said Derek, addressing Lucerne. 'You can put him in.'

Realizing that within moments she would escape, the nurse moved forward to see John move into fridge number four, third rack down. As she scouted with eyes the place where he would rest Derek stepped towards her and said approvingly, 'That's it.'

And she could see not only the bodies above and below but also to each side behind doors three and five. As the tray slid forward off the jacked-up trolley, Derek encouraged Lucerne, 'That's it, that's it – there next to the wee one,' and Lucerne saw that John would rest on a tray next to the body of a small, small child.

REVOLUTIONS 3

Dark night over sea and land. Night without a breath of dawn and the sea meeting the land and the river under the moon. Land holding the estuary and the water cold steel under a sky without warmth. The suburbs placid dormant strung thinly on the earth and in that house through a crack in the curtains the night sky only.

Where, up towards the angels, the scudding clouds cross the white orb and their frayed edges illuminated call torn flesh and the void that is all pain. Beyond this night and further than the surge of single tide, past days and into months and years that small window glimpse of the heavens where the gods inflict this. To live now is to leave the stench of this room, this planet and to tie the last of self to the angels playing out there in the skies through the only window there is.

Down in the suburb Dr Jones moved. He moved through his property from room to room. His rational mind alive and calculating and his body heated and full functioning and his soul just ready to die.

Sue rode on the alcohol and Alan began building his second joint of tobacco and marijuana. He could see Sue loosen with the drink and as she sat on a dining chair she swung her crossed leg. His mind played through its repertoire of pornography. He threw his eyes at her, at her face, at her breasts and at her thighs just exposed where her robe fell off her crossed legs. When she stood up, he caught sight of her briefs over her crotch.

She turned her back and stood adjusting the volume on the tape, shifting from foot to foot. Alan stood and lit his smoking confection. He moved behind her and put a hand on her hip. Sue flexed back a touch and buttocks brushed his jean trousered groin.

'Gonna have fun, baby.'

And she moved a little nervously and glanced back briefly, Maybe… are we?'

And Alan looked a little lost for a moment and then kicked off his trainers and undid his jeans by three buttons and walked towards her. Sue realised he was coming and would touch her and looked at his eyes and he looked back and then he was straight in front of her, his head one foot away. He found her eyes and his hand found her robe and moved and inside her underwear found her and she fell forward on his shoulder. She did not want to kiss him as she melted an aching slackness onto his hand. No more Will.

The morgue was locked and undisturbed. Derek Gerrard had deposited the keys in the porters' lodge with Webb, the senior night porter, who had signed the book. And then Derek Gerrard went. Webb would most probably not need them as nighttime deceased were generally left peacefully until morning.

The flesh in the fridges lay attached to the sorrow and grief of here by family and friends and by their love. Each collection of bones and organ and skin and capillary lay also in the hearts of the grieving and the sorrowful.

This night under the concrete hospital, in the bowels of a building of death and disease John's flesh lay cold and unnamed and unknown. There were no plans for him, no funeral, no oration, no prayer. His dead toes and dead eyes and still hardening blood lay unwanted.

The machinery hummed.

The angels loved Yolanda. They loved her as they held her as she held them while down on earth the pain of man was spent in the flesh. And up between the stars and everything beyond them, far beyond the sight of any mortal wound they flew over sea and mountain like clouds on the mountain, like rain in the wind and there was always from up there the first sight of dawn.

There was no backward glance into the fetid boxroom from the arms of angels, no fear of what now, only the surging joy of dawn here and another day, another day.

Sue panted as Alan explored her with his finger. Her arms hung around his neck and her head propped her chin on his shoulder. Alan stooped a little as his digit hooked inside and a bit higher. She had become from his first touch utterly open. He began to extract his finger and she began to grip it and judder and he lurched back his torso and took his shoulder from her chin and looked at her eyes and withdrew it and pulled on his joint and asked, 'Are we going to have fun?' as he stepped back from her.

She took up her drink and finished it. And refilled it and sipped again. Her legs were shaky. Her robe was undone. The whole room smelt of sex. She was dripping wet. She ached. Alan was still standing there.

Putting down her glass she walked over to him and close.

He reached for her hand and placed it on his prick outside his jeans. She looked up at his face and caught him unawares contemplating only his spliff. She squeezed and he looked at her and he smiled. He dragged deep on the joint and she undid the buttons and pulled his dick free and she felt it and he smiled at her and she went down stooping and then on her knees in front of him and taking it with licks and kisses into her mouth she began to drown out the last cries of Will.

Not one care or thought or word for John. The steel tomb throbbing with cold and the smell of chemical anninilation and all night the machinery hummed and Lucerne slept. Through the night the hospital worked at a low energy torpor, just a percentage of its daytime scurry. It took in the damaged and the dead and held them and mostly it watched while most slept.

Downstairs, double locked behind double doors, lay the new last generation and across all the towns and cities, through all villages and everywhere there lay not one single concern for the flesh and the bones lying on the tray behind door four third one down.

Another day, just a hint of not quite so dark and another day given by the angels to taste the sun. This dawn bearing up brought the first day that the angels gave Yolanda, the first day since her father had murdered his soul.

Gwen supervised breakfast awash on a stream of toxins. It would take less than an hour to get the children and her husband out of the house and then she would return to her bed and sleep into recovery.

Miranda told her, 'Yolanda won't get up.'

And Gwen screeched, 'Yolanda!' from the bottom of the stairs.

Miranda said again, 'She won't wake up.'

'I'll go,' volunteered Richard Jones in his crisp shirt and tie and he went up the stairs puffing with frustration.

Miranda and Adrian ate cereal in the kitchen. They were dependent on their big sister for their escort to school and knew that neither their mother nor their father would greet the responsibility of taking them there with anything less than annoyance. Their lives and needs were generally a nuisance.

'Go and brush your hair,' Gwen told Miranda and her daughter took herself away to seek out a brush. Adrian had spilt a spoon of milk and cereal on his tie and shirt and was rubbing at it ineffectively with a disposable cloth. Gwen saw him and expressed a groan of dissatisfaction and then intervened roughly.

Miranda came back half-heartedly pulling a brush through her hair.

'Not in the kitchen,' Gwen snapped, and the child turned back and stood in the doorway. Gwen gazed out of the window at the morning in the garden, her back turned on the routine of family life. Typically, Richard had left glasses and drinks on the table by the pool and she would have to go and retrieve them. Her resentment built up as a piece of cutlery clattered on the floor and she flinched as she heard her husband thudding down the stairs

After the children and Richard had left, Gwen would have to go and get the glasses and drinks and bring them in and wash them with the breakfast things. Then she would have to go upstairs to get dressed. She would have hardly any time before the children were back from school.

Dr Jones appeared in the kitchen, 'She's throwing a temperature – I'll have to give her something.'

Gwen turned round to see her husband going back into the hall and opening the door to the study.

Miranda and Adrian watched him going upstairs with his square leather medical bag. Yolanda's mother seethed now as she perceived her children's needs conspiring to inflict further and escalating demands on her.

More than anything Gwen hated the morning school gate scene. Somehow there always seemed to be one parent or another giving her a critical viewing. Even when she dropped Miranda and Adrian off by car there always seemed to be someone staring accusingly, looking at her questioningly. And if Yolanda was ill, she, Gwen, would have to drop the other two down there.

Last time this had been imposed on her the whole day had become unbearable. She remembered the awful man shouting at her about her driving and the looks from the ordinary mums. Gwen had at one stage taken off her sunglasses but then had put them back on when a rather fat young woman with a posse of kids had caught her gaze.

She felt bitter about Richard letting Hannah go now. For an au pair Hannah was a reasonable girl.

Gwen saw her husband had come back downstairs. He was fiddling with his medical bag, relocating its contents and closing it up. He glanced up and at her. Miranda and Adrian were just standing around. Dr Richard Jones stood up and delivered his diagnosis to Gwen as he slipped into his car coat with its raised collar and elasticated cuffs. 'She's picked up something pretty unpleasant. Probably from that filthy stables.' He knew too well what Gwen's concerns would be.

'She should sleep most of the day now. I'll drop the other two off.'

Gwen still struggling to function felt the necessity to inflict her sense of resentment. 'If I still had help. If you hadn't told Hannah to go.'

Dr Jones walked up close to his wife. His face was inches from hers. Through an almost locked jaw he told her, 'Shut up.'

He walked away. Then turned back and got up close to her face. Through the locked jaw and under his breath her told her, 'Hannah was lovely.'

The tide flooded upriver into the city and the city lay under the phosphorous lights and by the first hints of dawn Alan had laid into Sue three times the power of his youth. From the panoply of images from his squirreled stock of hardcore publishing he had, without love, taken her.

She had held her head on the sofa, forward on her knees, as he had driven into her. Gasping as he pounded her from behind, her breasts slapping forward, sweat popping on her back. His hands pulling her apart and his self pushing into her. Up into her and her mouth gaped open and he pushed again and again.

Alan leant back and admired his own hot action, watched himself slipping in and out and in and looked at her devouring him. From his back through his buttocks to his thighs his muscles locked almost rigid in the drive of desire. He half pulled out and rested a moment from the rhythm and teased with small twitches and she sighed with a want to fill the ache, the grief now of a lost Will.

'Good,' and, 'Nice,' he told her, and hinted at an increased movement. And she sighed and pushed her hand down and to the flexing by playing gently with her clitoris. And he increased his in and pulled out a little more and teasing at her wanting, kept asking, 'Is it good? Do you want more?' and played through the scenes with a dialogue constructed from the porn scenes he watched.

Leaning forward over her he cupped her right breast and pulled at the nipple.

With a grimace she said, 'Be careful,' and he pounded harder at her again, angrily from behind until she became lost and her hair matted her forehead and her whole body rocked forward with his push.

Then he pulled out and laid her on her back on the carpet and on his knees entered her – looking at her eyes which she shut. Determinedly he pushed in and out of her, and on and on with all the endurance of youth.

Sue took it with pleasure and then as it became almost mechanical it waned, physically less, but came back again and again as he went on and on. She sent her hand down to feel his strength and his hardness and wanting him released now she played with him adding more with her fingers.

Sue held his balls and made a ring round his cock with her finger and thumb and pulled at him and he seemed to expand into her and she pulled on at him. He drove harder at her again and again and Sue took her hand and hooked at his hard belly with her nails as he filled her and she pulled at him and he washed her with warmth.

He pulled straight out and naked, stood up over her and with false certainty pronounced, 'You're not bad,' and strutted over to the table with the drink and poured himself one and after a moment looked for her glass to get one for her too.

Sue rolled over for her robe. Her underwear was lost. Once covered she stayed sat on the carpet watching Alan and accepting the drink he offered her. He looked for his stash of tobacco and marijuana and finished his drink in two takes. He poured himself some more and began to roll a joint. Sue just watched.

Alan bragged about his sexual adventures and drank and Sue drank and he repeated he'd *do anything* and how he was going to make a porn film and how he knew what he was doing. With the drink Sue let him speak uninterrupted and unlistened and she watched the flex of his chest as he moved on the dining chair. She sat half reclined on the couch and he filled her glass at intervals and she now happily shared joints with him.

Will was gone and this young man was dulling her out on the booze and the dope and as he fell preoccupied in some story about some girl and playing again with the dope. Sue let her legs fall open and let her hand feel there the warmth of his come as it fell out of her. In her openness her finger felt her own wet mixed with his and she felt the edge of delight still there.

Half closing her eyes she let go and drifted and then came back as she heard a catch in his voice. She looked at him, only half focused, and saw that he had seen her moves and was unnerved. Challenged his voice was a touch brittle as he said, 'Go on then,' and she closed her eyes again and for a moment let her head loll back. Again, glimpsing him she now saw and felt his reinterest.

Her robe open, her legs open, herself open Sue lay only with some physical pleasure for comfort. Strcking her pulsing self, touching her only beating self she lay there and he looked at her as he looked at the magazine images and with the same eyes that looked on the frames of flesh films he consumed. Stirred now, Alan brought himself back into frame, walking across to the couch and standing over her full and erect in his own hand. Pulling the robe fully away from her breasts he breathed, 'I am going to come on you baby,' and Sue half opened her eyes to see him there over her, above her.

Half opening her mouth she gestured towards her lips, 'Bring it here,' and guided Alan's dick into her mouth.

Helpless he gave it to her and she held him and controlled him as she fed it into her face, into her mouth and onto the edge of her throat.

With him quiet, Sue let herself go and played in her wetness and in her mind was wild and wilder and wilder. And it went on and on with his hands in her hair and on her breasts and his hand tracing her arm down to her hand and joining with her there.

He put her on the floor and rode her again. Harder than before, fighting through her fatigue with tens of minutes of rigid strokes.

Lost, she could only brace herself against him with her hands above her head pushed into the base of the settee. He could rock forward and go deeper down into her or rock back and go up into her and he could pound at her or tease gently at her and her lips lay flaccid on her teeth as she breathed through the night.

Drunk and high and unwashed she took her daughters to school. Riding on flashback memories she walked away from the gates and back towards her home. She remembered how she'd lain completely open with no strength left in her thighs, her legs almost still as he had taken her completely and finally spilled into her.

She must have dozed there on the carpet as the sky lightened with dawn. But hardly for long because he had come down beside her and she had got herself sat up with her robe over her shoulders. He sat close to her, cross-legged, both of them naked. Dry mouthed and worn out, her mouth wanted the drink he offered and her body took it craving some sustenance. She drank and her system came alive and he offered her, 'Sue you're fantastic,' and her self lifted and he drank his drink and smoked and she smoked and drank and the sky lightened more.

He put down his glass and outed the joint and went behind her and kissed her neck and played gently with her nipples. She tried a laugh of, 'I don't think I can,' but he responded with an increased urgency on her breasts and rocked her down sideways onto the floor. She lay on her side and he lay behind her stroking her breasts with his prick throbbing against her buttocks.

His lips kissed her neck and she tried, 'I'm tired, I think…' and he put his hand on her arse and then between her legs and pushed her forward onto her front and his fingers played in the wetness of what had gone before. Kissing her neck, he pushed against her and her weariness and laid his pulsing prick between buttocks. He rocked it back and forth and his fingers played in her.

She had said, 'Don't, Alan don't.' But he had leant more weight on her and she could feel a terrible heat from him as he spread the come and the wet onto her tight hole and began probing at her with his prick.

'Don't, I don't want to.'

And he pushed two fingers into her wet hole and leant harder on her back and pulled out from her his fingers dripping and spread the wetness onto her tight hole. Then probing at it he took his hand to his mouth and dripped spit into his palm.

He leant over her completely, his mouth by her ear and rubbed his whole hand from front to back between her legs and told her, 'I love it in the dirtbox.'

Sue walked home from the school with a stagger from the drink and the drugs and with a burning deep unease inside her. The last of that putrid dry heat in her and the sun blazed on the white concrete. After his final act she had hardly waited, just regained her composure before she recovered herself enough to tell him, 'Go.'

His moment's hesitation melted as he saw just her animal self rise to, 'Now.'

And in minutes he was gone.

Three teenagers trailed past on early patrol for their day's narcotic fix and Sue walked home.

Derek Gerrard parked his motorbike in the hospital car park and entered the building still dressed in the all in one protective overall and carrying his full-face helmet. He picked up the keys from the porters' lodge by the main entrance and made his way directly to the staff canteen on lower ground one. Walking heavily in biker boots he unzipped his suit from neck to sternum and picked up a coffee from the self-service bar.

He went down to the morgue and let himself in through the doors and began to settle himself down in his office. He sipped at his coffee as he changed into his green surgical garb and hung up his biker gear. There was a large desk diary and a mechanical tape telephone answer machine on his desk. Also there was the mortuary ledger and a holder for pens, pencils and paperclips. Derek Gerrard always kept his desk tidy and clear.

He played the answer phone and found there were no messages overnight and recorded the new message for the new day using his nonchalant, *Hello this is the morgue* introduction. There were no visitors booked until eleven am. It was a straightforward visit from a family of a deceased. Generally things were far busier than this and generally Derek Gerrard had more opportunity to exert his power. A quiet morning, a quiet day and his chances to strut were diminished.

He reviewed the ledger and noted the incomplete entry for John. Irritatingly it was unresolved and no solution came to his mind. However, an issue had been identified and taking up an issue gave the morgue porter an energy and a purpose.

The hospital stood up twelve floors from the sprawl of surrounding housing. It gathered in traffic, motorised and pedestrian, a magnet to labour and the ill.

It took in all this humanity and in its halls and corridors

they moved between theatre, ward, X-ray and transport, between pharmacy and radiology, between laundry and patient affairs. Closing the morgue with relish Derek Gerrard set off to resolve the issue of the unidentified soul lying in the fridge.

REVOLUTIONS 4

Rivers, estuaries, seas, oceans. Oceans on a planet spinning a rotation and making days, making months. The moon pushing tides, neaps and springs, through calendars marking time where no human action can challenge the movements through space. Onward, unstoppable days after hours and never certainty. The city with dust holes where the tallest buildings stood, the ruins of civilisations spotted from space.

What is gone is yesterday and held memory a wave on the shore, a mark at high tide. It's all lost now. No revisitation, no second chance – it is all consumed by the clock – no memory can undo or reconstruct those times now gone. Out in the estuary soft sand and mud delve gently into the sea that laps wavelets at their slightest inclines. Tumbling sand grains and the tide falls and there are rippled scars across the mud as far as you can see.

One day you open your eyes and it is your last day on earth and all that has gone before is gone. You cannot know memory is different from dreams, you cannot know hardly anything at all. Certainty is vapourised, you cannot know it was true.

Yolanda, a woman past thirty, safe in the city laughing with friends, wine in her hand. Her body is strong from hot beaches and warm seas and she is strong in her intent. On a mountain, the wind in her hair, a cloud crosses the sun and the shadow scoots on the hillside a dark flutter like memory.

Gwen got up again at lunchtime. She took a light lunch with her glass of wine and jumped when the phone rang. It was Richard who spoke factually, 'I will pick up Miranda and Adrian. Have you spoken to Yolanda?'

'No, she's still sleeping,' said Gwen avoicing the question and giving her husband peace of mind. It was most unusual for Richard to telephone or to accommodate domestic arrangements but Gwen chewed at her sandwich indifferently. Richard had in place the entire family routine and it ran by her generally unnoticed. She thought she would remember to go back upstairs to look at her daughter.

Outside a magpie stood on the edge of the lawn looking under the rosebushes. Gwen looked through her window seeking its mate. 'One for sorrow, two for joy,' she half muttered and flushed with relief when she spotted the other one of the pair. Monogamous mates, the magpies, tied for life like her and Richard.

A light aircraft droned over the suburb and smart new cars parked in the supermarket car park. There was a good railway connection to the city and the churches stood proud among the shops and businesses. It was one place like so many scattered around and beyond the edge of the city.

Sue got back into her house and looked at the mess. It really wasn't too bad, ashtrays and glasses and dishevelled furniture, some stray underwear by the settee. In forty minutes it was all put right and the washing machine tumbled with clothes. The girls had not woken, they had not come downstairs, and in the morning mummy had been there alone. They had hardly noticed the shambles in the rush out to school.

Sue sat on the settee with a cup of tea and a cigarette and felt the tiredness in her bones. Closing her eyes allowed scenes from last night to rush into her consciousness and restless she stood up and went up the straight flight of stairs into the bathroom. Using a shower attached to the bath taps she washed herself functionally before crashing out on the bed she once shared with Will. Sue made sure she tidied Sharon's and Emma's beds and toys.

Asleep Sue could rest from the recall of the sweat and the odour and rest from the worry of consequence and reaction. And Alan slept too and he slept easy and comfortable. When he stirred and half came conscious, he grinned and smirked with the satisfaction of conquest.

'Thanks for popping in, Derek,' said Pat Driscombe, 'I've got a note and will let you know.'

'OK, Pat,' said Derek Gerrard lifting himself off of the seat opposite the Head of Patient Affairs.

'I thought I'd better let you know.'

'Of course, Derek, many thanks,' said Pat, who had a range of reassuring motherly tones always at her disposal. She wanted the lumpen morgue porter out of her office. The management of the mortuary was absolutely not her responsibility and the unbearable Derek Gerrard had no business in her office.

Now on his feet Derek could better leverage the conversation as he looked at Pat Driscombe. Behind her desk she was all bosom and blouse and her sagging middle-aged features propped up large rimmed spectacles. Pat was fifty and overweight and wheezy from her twenty-five cigarettes a day. Her job incorporated the handling of the property of the dead and the liaison with the families of the deceased and with the undertakers and all concerned.

Derek made towards the door and then turned back and addressed her.

'The thing is, Pat, anything could happen to him, there's no record, no number, no notes.'

'Of course it's concerning, Derek.'

Derek walked three paces across the room towards her window. On his feet he was roaming her territory. He knew she wanted him gone.

'It's more than concerning, Pat. It's a situation that is out of control.'

'Well leave it with me,' said Pat, viewing the flabby physique of the man in her office. His belly swelled forwards from his chest and his flabbed arms sloped out from his falling shoulders. Pat wondered whether he could be forbidden from wearing the surgical green trousers and shirt. The situation with this body did not concern her at all. She was sure that by the end of the week she would be dealing with some grief-stricken relatives desperate to find out if the dead man had any money.

'It's all very well for you to say that, Pat, sitting here all day.' Derek was beginning to feel better. 'Sitting here all day you're not hands on, so to speak.'

The *Sitting here all day* was satisfying Derek and aggravating Pat. Her face flushed and hardened, 'Derek, sitting here all day I deal with every trauma and tragedy you can imagine.'

He was resting against the window sill looking steadily at her agitation. 'Of course you do, Pat, and none of us can afford to make mistakes.'

Pat was trained to absorb anger. It sort of shot into her surplus flesh. She didn't recoil from the hysterical accusations from the newly bereaved, from the anger of loss. Her stolid stoic frame endured the wounded cries of the grief-struck and got through the necessary administration. Pat admired those who maintained their manners and dignity and exorcised her own resentment on those who wailed. Pat could say, *I realise you must be upset*, to the weeping relatives of a deceased and riddle it with sarcasm.

'Are you going back to your place of work now, Derek?' she said tapping at her computer keyboard. 'I am sure you must have much to be going on with.'

She sat in an office and he worked in the basement with fridges of dead people. Derek stretched his arms up behind his bloated neck and affected a worldly sigh. His eyes were small in the flesh of his face as he surveyed the desk and chair and office of his colleague. Of course he felt not one drop of envy for her position or environment, she was not after all, hands on like him.

'You're right, Pat, I must get on. Thanks for your time.' He moved towards the door.

'OK, Derek.'

But the porter half turned back. He fixed her eyes in a rigid stare. 'You're welcome to come down, Pat. I'd leave you alone with him.'

Richard Jones breezed in with Miranda and Adrian in happy family man mode. He announced, 'Special super Jones pizzas later – go and play now – upstairs.' as his two younger children trailed in the door after him. He found Gwen walking towards him from the kitchen and he strode up to her and laid a hand on her shoulder and a k ss on her cheek. 'Darling,' he said, as he assessed her wine laden breath and rheumy eyes. Gwen's face held a broken smile and he was past her into the kitchen.

Gwen followed Richard as he opened the fridge and the dishwasher. This quick survey reassured him that Gwen had followed her usual pattern for daytimes. He turned and addressed her, 'I had a word with Dominic and he says you have to be pretty careful with some of these farmyard viruses. I got some antibiotics from the pharmacy and told the school she won't be back until next week. Oh, and I called the agency about a replacement for Hannah.'

Gwen loved her Richard and loved his efficiency and effectiveness and organisation. Of course a powerful man like him got frustrated and irritable when she let him down. His little explosions never lasted and he gave her everything and always took care of her. She was the wife of a man with considerable status and power and she needed to play her part and do what was required. And the way Richard structured everything there were few trying obligations and generally without exception he was in charge. Also, this way, they never argued – at all.

Dr and Mrs Jones attended professional and community (particularly church) events and Richard was pleased to relate his views on various things. His wife,

Gwen, had her hands full with three little horrors and he would glean information from polite conversation. He was completely dismissive of those of lesser station and would even move away in mid-sentence. Those who he perceived to hold higher position would find Richard Jones nodding acquiescence at their shoulder. He was highly successful at work.

The doorbell was ringing louder and louder. Louder and trying to breakthrough a cottonwool barrier of sleep until Sue jolted awake. As she sought out the clock with her sticky eyes, she could hear her children's voices through the letterbox downstairs shouting, 'Mummy.'

It was thirty-five minutes after picking up time from the school and she had slept on unknowing. She shouted 'Coming,' and put on her baggy trousers and loose top and went down to greet them.

Opening the door, she picked up the big smiling Emma while Sharon pushed past with a rebuke laden, 'Oh mummy.' This had never happened before.

Standing up straight with younger daughter still in her arms Sue saw that it was Natalie Farrell who had brought them down. Natalie was smoking a cigarette and pushing a buggy back and forwards with her other hand and looking just slightly smug.

'Thanks, Natalie.'

'No problem, Sue.'

Natalie was about the same age as Sue and a little overweight, a mother of three who lived in the next block without the support of any man.

'When I saw them still there, I just told the teacher

you'd asked me to take them down with mine.'

It was a lie constructed to protect Sue's reputation at the school and she was grateful to Natalie for it. They had never even passed time together before as Sue's aspirations had always excluded those with less. Natalie puffed on her cigarette and looked at Sue with a little hard edge to her expectancy. She was almost daring Sue to close the door on her now. With her daughters returned and safe indoors there was some part of Sue that wanted it shut and Natalie gone, but she felt the candour of neediness from the woman who had just helped her out and she said, 'Natalie thanks. Do you want to come in for a moment.'

Natalie was delighted to be inside Sue's house, to see the carpets and furniture and the way everything matched and was new. Her toddler, Barnaby, was asleep in the buggy, a bottle of orange juice in the crook of his arm. The middle boy Jason was *Playing with his mates* and her eldest *Does as he pleases now*. Natalie had begun her family when she was sixteen and each boy was from a different man.

Sue made them a cup of tea and Natalie struggling to find friendship asked Sue questions that did not sometimes require an answer but carried flattery or expressed admiration. Sue found the simple, 'Don't you think your house is lovely?' 'Don't you think your girls look lovely?' reassuring and as she warmed to Natalie she opened a new packet of the expensive chocolate biscuits.

Sharon and Emma began to agitate for their tea and Barnaby woke up as the two women began to edge towards a mutual acceptance. Natalie began to make her exit as soon as her son became restive and knowing that she had succeeded in reaching out to Sue she wanted to avoid causing irritation or annoyance. Sue was pleased she was going but conscious that her warmth would be leaving her alone with a long evening ahead. She was surprised when she found herself saying, 'Are you doing anything later – why not pop round.'

And she was pleased when Natalie said she would if she could.

Derek Gerrard left Patient Affairs with his bizarre offer circulating before Pat Driscombe. It was some minutes before she could accept how he had left her with such an insult and degradation. Then the image began to solidify and the unspoken possibilities emerged and she shuddered.

The morgue porter smirked a little upon leaving and set himself a course to find Staff Nurse Lucerne. His gait was half shuffle and half traipse as his overweight frame made its way through corridors and lifts. He passed by the wheelchairs carrying thin weak human frames some of whom grasped their own urine in clear plastic bags. In the lift he did not see the man with the yellow skin and chemical baldness or the child who was fading away.

An old lady trembled on a chair waiting for a test, her ulcered legs bandaged and her veins pulsing under translucent skin while a grey man in a dressing gown made for the door clutching the cigarettes that had finished him. This Asian woman on crutches and a broad pregnant African, and a stretcher rigged with fluid bags draining into a struggling body. The hospital sang with its work and eased the pain of the dying and fought on to sustain life. Disease always reaped with terrible democracy.

The hospital workers were paid less than others as if

the karma gains were somehow calculated on a monetary scale. Close up to the puss, the tumour, the infected, these men and women took less. And things could go wrong on the most terrible scale when mad medics unsupervised implemented treatment programmes that killed year after year while the cleaners and orderlies and assistants and technicians worked day after day after night.

Above the hospital chimney the sky at least was sterile blue above the paltry aspirations below. Waste and washing were sluiced and processed and there was birth, admission, death and release in the strange stood-up oblong protruding from the other buildings around. There were red signs and arrows pointing towards Accident and Emergency and here Derek Gerrard expected to find Staff Nurse Lucerne.

'She's not down here anymore. She's back up on Baker,' he was told and he turned away from the chaotic hall surrounded by cubicles. He caught an interesting glimpse of a heavily shattered lower leg as he walked back out past triage. One of the rooms in X-ray threw out a volume of jarring groans and he stood aside as green-suited paramedics headed back to their vehicle pulling a now empty stretcher. He kicked aside a bloodied dressing that he saw by his foot.

In the lift there was an offer of a, FREE Makeover, sponsored by a charity for cancer sufferers and the morgue porter imagined that the public assumed he was a surgeon. Baker was a geriatric ward and was found on the tenth floor.

The matt silver lift doors opened and Derek Gerrard stepped out into the barely suppressed smell of old people's urine that coloured the air. He progressed down the corridor with his features alive and almost twitching, and his eyes searched out for the curves of Lucerne among the uniforms of nurses and domestics. Further down there was a commotion of agonising ghastly high- and low-pitched chilling scream groans emitting from a chair holding a twisted body with stone eyes jarring from random disassociated movement. The last throes of body without brain – where dementia has shrunk away all intelligent systems – but still no Lucerne.

Derek Gerrard circled back once more investing more time without asking in order to maintain his surprise. He wanted to catch her unawares and without protection. He wanted to see her. He wanted to see the fear.

A great warm ocean between continents warmed by the heat of our star and energy washing up onto beaches as breaking waves throw ribbons of surf onto the sand. Swells in the blue sea under skies clear of any distress and days like no other forever burnt with eternity. Hundreds and thousands of pink crabs scurry and hide from the feet of the fresh human youth alone here so far from city or suburb. Beat after heartbeat and wave after wave and young tumbling flesh playing in the washing warm waters.

Naked frolics beyond the sight of any human and sand on tanned flesh and bright coral grains in the fine down on your skin. Smile deeper than joy here. Days under the sun and muscle under the skin laying into the surf again and again. A swell, a wave, a flurry of arms and it holds you and carries you onto the beach.

As the golden orb begins to fall from the tropical sky there is a young woman walking the beach in a cloth of orange and gold wrapped under her arms and over her breasts falling almost to her feet. Her shoulders are strong, square-muscled and her hair sea-flattened to her head. The sand squeezes between her toes and she walks away from those days.

Memory now a celebration, a glory, recalling it a hymn to the beauty of those moments where youth could play free under the sun and the stars. Another day, another day from the angels and forever and ever. Two continents away from where they called it home Yolanda was free.

Natalie rang at Sue's door at nine pm with a bottle of the cheapest wine and Barnaby asleep in his pyjamas under a blanket in his pushchair. Jason was staying at Darren's and Natalie had bathed, washed her hair and changed into her clean jeans and T-shirt. Sue had brushed her hair and changed her top and put on a touch of make-up. Sue particularly appreciated the gesture with the wine. She knew how deep it would cut into Natalie's funds.

Sue opened the bottle and Natalie admired the glass she was given to drink from. It was from Sue's wedding present set. Sue quite bathed in Natalie's admiration and attention. By the time the bottle was empty the two women were laughing familiarly and as Natalie relaxed her easy humour emerged. More than anything she laughed at herself. Sue returned some of her flattery.

'Those jeans really suit you, Natalie.'

Natalie stood up and patted her broad backside looking down at her own flank.

'Thank you, Sue. Maybe if I get slim like you some bastard might stay with me – eh?'

'No, you look lovely.'

'Thanks. I bet you're missing your Will.'

'Well, yes and no.'

Natalie laughed.

'I know what I'm missing.'

And Sue laughed and Natalie told her in mock confidentiality, 'In my situation you've got take what you can get,' and they both laughed. Natalie felt Sue's slight discomfort with the more lurid direction of the conversation and giggled. 'I get my fun – don't you worry,' and Sue felt easier with her openness and the previous night's activity flashed through her mind.

The wine was finished for some time before Sue felt the evening beginning to drag and she offered, 'Fancy more wine, Natalie?'

And her new friend giggled, 'I'm not an alcoholic but I'm not saying no.'

And Sue went to the cupboard and Natalie couldn't help her eyes following Sue's hand into the cupboard and onto the money.

Natalie had pulled on her jacket and was saying, 'It's OK, I'll go,' as Sue handed her five pounds. Natalie looked at the money and said, 'You got any lemonade?'

And Sue said 'Yes.'

And Natalie pushed her hand into her jeans' pocket pulling out some change and said, 'You can get a bottle of vodka for seven pounds round there,' and hesitated not knowing if she'd gone too far.

Sue laughed and said, 'Alright then, girls' night in, might as well,' and went back to the cupboard and pulled out ten pounds which she put in Natalie's hand pulling back the five pound note.

'I don't need all that,' said Natalie.

'Don't worry – get cigarettes too,' said Sue.

Natalie went out into the night onto the concrete between the rows of maisonettes piled block upon block across this corner of the city. Deep thudding music came from somewhere nearby and as Natalie walked up the ramp out of the estate a fast flicker of light illuminated the faces of Alan and Tony and Ben as they gathered around smoking the pungent weed hearing the tale told of the previous night.

Staff Nurse Lucerne was taking the pulse of eighty-three-year-old Lettie Smith who was a new admission to Baker Ward. The nurse sat quietly on the bedside chair, her eyes focused on the watch pinned to the top of her apron. Lettie Smith was a small bony frame propped half upright on four hospital pillows her legs angular rods under the blanket. Lucerne's healthy fleshed fingers sat lightly on the tiny ancient wrist feeling every heartbeat. Lettie's slightly reedy voice spoke with complete intellectual control.

'I don't think I will be able to put up with it. Nothing against you but I don't think I can take it in here.'

'Well, we'll get you out of here soon enough.'

Lucerne put down her wrist and entered the figures on the chart.

'I don't think so,' said Lettie 'I keep falling over at home. I can't get into bed now. The home help is scared to come around in case I'm lying there dead.'

'Well…'

'No. I might as well be now. I might as well be I'm all worn out. A bloody burden.'

There were tears in Lettie's eyes and damaged pride in her voice. Lucerne loved the pride, the value of independence that this woman had achieved. The nurse held her one hand while the old lady dabbed at her face with a tissue in the other. It was quiet for a moment and then Lettie took back her hand from the nurse and reached for a small toilet bag on the cabinet beside her bed. Her tiny ancient fingers opened the zip and located a compact which she struggled for a moment to open. Lucerne watched as Lettie Smith repaired her make up in the small round mirror.

Richard Jones imitated the brusque manner of the nurses he had observed as he dealt with the situation in Yolanda's room that evening. He prepared a tray of warmed tinned soup and bread with a drink of juice to wash down the tablets. He called Miranda and said, 'Go with her to the loo, she's still feeling woozy,' while he pulled off the bedclothes that needed changing. The older girl looked at her younger sister and wobbled away. When the bed was done he got a clean nightdress and took it down to the toilet.

As his eldest girl stood up from the seat he said, 'Put this on,' and waited as she did. She was unsteady and uncertain on her feet. He picked up the one she had been wearing and went back and picked up the dirty bedclothes and threw them in a pile. Yolanda came down the hall holding Miranda's hand.

'Well done,' he said, and, 'Go on and play then,' to his youngest and he put Yolanda in bed with pillows behind her and the tray with the soup on her knees. He sat on the bed and told her, 'You've had a high temperature and have been running a fever. Don't worry the tablets will get rid of it.'

His daughter looked mostly vacant and non-functioning, unresponsive to his voice. He told her, 'It's a nasty virus. From the stables I expect. Don't worry. It might give you funny dreams though.'

Dr Richard Jones left the room and was gone from Yolanda who slowly put down the tray and then lay unmoved as dusk turned to night and the night sky appeared through the crack in the curtains. Still as it was grey washes of slow hardly changing cloud lay like negative shadows across the heavens on a plane below the moon. Beyond that the stars.

Natalie came back and she and Sue drank all the vodka too quickly and Sue had soon told Natalie about her thing with Alan. Natalie was quite admiring of her new friend's adventure and also encouraging of the openness of disclosure and blatant in her enjoyment of any carnal detail.

Giggling she asked, 'Go on then – how many times?' and her mirth was infectious and Sue laughed too. Taking it all as ludicrous comedy safely diminished it and reduced all consequence.

'I saw him just now,' said Natalie.

'Oh my God,' groaned Sue in exaggerated horror.

Still giggling Natalie said, 'He's very fit, Sue. Tell him I'm waiting if you can't take any more.'

Sue laughed with genuine relief now as the punctured secrecy dissipated the power of the events. Natalie's crudeness was a comfort and reassurance as if she could indeed take on or share the burden of a man's sexual demands.

It wasn't late and the two women sat on the cushions on the sitting room floor sharing an ashtray and still laughing when they were suddenly silenced by a ring on the doorbell. Flushed and excited Natalie could barely hold down her voice as she leant over to Sue almost bursting with excitement.

'That's him – I bet that's him.'

Staff Nurse Lucerne looked out of the window. The hospital management had strung a net over the floors below with the intention of catching the suicides from psychiatry on floor twelve. Sometimes Lucerne struggled with the absurd and ridiculous intentions of man to mess with the ways of the gods. Every day death defeated the finest minds and every day birth laid a miracle before logic and intellect and when on her knees Lucerne prayed in true awe of this power. From the windows of Baker Ward you could see some miles over the rooftops to the core of the city or out towards where green began to break up the grey. Out there the actions of man, with all its self-importance and pride, were so little when you looked up at the sky. Lucerne absently watched the shifting clouds expanding and distending and metamorphosing against the blue and then she began to watch only the blue. One patch of blue as deep as the universe and she smiled with the peace of the moment.

The rubber surgeon's theatre shoes were silent on the polished and buffed hospital floor.

'What shall I do with this body?' asked Derek Gerrard.

REVOLUTIONS 5

It is night on the east coast. At the water's edge the sea beats against the shingle. Behind the banked beach are low marshes inhabited by caravans and beyond that farms, villages, towns, and cities. The sky is splattered with high stars.

It's dark now. Looking out over the moving sea there is no horizon. Or maybe just a hint of light on a line at the limit of sight. And on the beach a youth, a being at the moment when childhood departs, when the body is fully formed, but without one atom of decay.

Now out there across the sea against all that dark a vague greying of the shadows. Out there over the water against the furthest cavity of black a softening of light. An easing of the infinity, a precursor of dawn.

The horizon lightens and the clouds catch silver against the black and a line emerges where sea meets sky. On the beach the youth sits on the bench and watches the first shreds of dawn. It's a grasp of that time as the sea kisses the shore and the earth spins down to allow up the light. A yellowing of the spreading grey and objects emerge from the dimness and a thickening of the light against clouds and then the breaking of the dark. A first gentle blast of orange shard underlining a line of sky and light and shade delineating the earth. On her feet the breathing being stretching against the cold air and standing, the elevation gives us the first sight of the slightest edge of our star.

The planet drops the horizon spinning down and inch by inexorable inch the orange globe nudges up and across the sea, and up into the sky and everywhere the merest gentlest immeasurable draft of warmth. Up it comes an endless deep pit of glowing heat and dissolving the dark, light spreading across sky, across sea, across land. Shadows appearing and by the minutest degree, heat, warmth, life coming.

The youth walks and dawn blazes from the sun, across now golden seas and pink liveried clouds and the black is now more blue. She walks as the sea lilts on the sand and splashes on the stones and the day is born as every day is born.

This one dawn is marked and remembered but dawn is every day. Now for this girl, now just woman, this moment is burnt into her, a memory that stays and lasts.

A dawn, alone on the beach. No triumph or disaster, no company, no man or woman just a time when clarity is gifted and the world drowns you with marvel and beauty. And the witness to all this is a body perfect with youth. No rot or corruption, tiredness or age, a body and a spirit that is free from all that has gone before and free from all that is to come.

The young woman is not yet twenty but that time has passed. Gone forever like the night. She sets off jogging with the sun round, fully raised, clear of the sea. Her feet push off the grass at the back of the beach. Her knees rise lifting her thighs and lengthening her stride, opening her lungs.

Shifting across the landscape she covers five

kilometres in thirty minutes. A measured course set against time. Not like histories buried away in the dark before dawn. Hidden back in the days before this day that sees her shoulders rise and fall and the breath that feeds the blood with oxygen. The morning air in her lungs new in the minutes after dawn.

Now the stones glint washed by the sea and wet in the sun, now the sky is all blue with pure white clouds high in the near space. She rocks along gliding through the metres, one after another and the minutes tick on.

Always on. The earth spinning towards the heat and everyday a sunrise and always on and always on – and never back. Each step another metre, another second, and nothing left now of that night. Nothing left of that dark. Nothing.

This girl runs on the grass behind the beach alongside the road. Looking around she sees a magpie searching the gutter. A magpie alone. *One for sorrow* she thinks, her legs stretching between paces her eyes scanning ahead. She spots a second bird on a fence post *two for joy* and then a third *three for a girl* and its companion *four for a boy*.

She is heading towards the town. There are more birds ahead. Again magpies. *Five for silver* she murmurs, and then she sees one more *six for gold* she says out loud, *six for gold* she says out loud between hard breaths.

Her cheeks are red but she is not struggling. The bright morning is a crystal moment of beauty. She finds her thoughts flying with her strides, her steps pounding the questions into her mind. Questions that have always been there. The why, the big why to what is it that happened. Her mum, her mother. Why.

Her head dips, there's another bird. Its eyes black and

beady without humanity. The gloss and sheen of its plumage suddenly sickly under the sun. *Seven*, she mutters, *for a story never to be told*.

In the city you could buy anything. Anything you could think of. The city was placed where the sea became land, where the great ocean became a sea, an estuary a tidal reach and up into the heart of the land where the sun fed the earth. Here where water lapped on mucous mud everything could be changed, exchanged, bought and sold.

There were the great towers of glass and concrete, the phalluses of commerce, of money lenders' empires. There were tiny alcove shops retailing packets of tobacco and bars of sugar. The mighty world girdling organisations retailing all the goods that man has ever wanted and single men selling sheaves of printed paper for pennies.

In this city you could buy the future and buy the past. You can buy what may happen in far off lands, the crops that have not been planted, the oil that has not been drilled. And you can buy art and objects from a thousand years ago.

The moon crosses the Atlantic Ocean and its force field swells the sea, swells water up the estuary and pushes it ripping up the river. Cargoes from everywhere ride up the river into the city and are bought and sold now by electric pulses as much as they were by a handshake before. A heaving mass has gathered here, a mass of humanity millions strong and everything is for sale.

There are cold places. Some super cold and some just chilled where man has tried to stop decay, to store the fruit to save it from decay, from time. The produce of sun-baked lands, fruit in all its colours, is held to be sold. And other fridges hold frozen water, ice, cold, to be sold for giving a chill to a rich man's drinks.

Somewhere in all this are cold places that hold the very substance of human existence. Among al the cold storage facilities, from fruit store to morgue, scmewhere man has a deep chill where the first cells of human life are stored. In the hospital where there is the morgue they also have chilled sperm and egg and embryo. You can buy life itself.

The city is all change, exchange, trade, rent, buy, and sell. In the heat of the night, you can buy or rent a human body for pleasure. You can buy a grave or precious metal or a musical tune or barrel of oil or a litre of petrol. Inland people can bring farm goods and seafarers' harvest from the sea or goods from far off lands. Everywhere is a market – a place for trade.

On the east coast a small ship, a barge, could nudge on top of the tide against a field that lay at the top of a creek. The barge would be loaded with hay, stacked in the hold and high on the deck. The tide would pull the wallowing barge away from the field, down the east coast river, ebbing away and out into the estuary. The tide changes and the flood gathers under the craft and sweeps it up into the city.

Before now, the hay would go to the Haymarket, to be sold. But not now. Now it goes somewhere else. Now the old names are redundant, surpassed by new markets, new trades, a different type of exchange.

But now in the Haymarket you can buy other things. Maybe stories. Maybe that man going into that office – that one millionth movement of man in the city in that minute is selling a story. Sparrows are rare; magpies are everywhere, *one for sorrow, seven for a story never to be told*.

Sue looked at the money. Sue thought of her girls, of Will, of the dark night. The shadow of Alan on her. The reek of body heat. Of sweat and discharge.

The hospital had a cash office. Staff Nurse Lucerne walked past. An office where money was taken to pay for things, for treatment, for drugs, for life and for things after life has been ended. Everything was priced and calculated. Nursing care per hour. Surgery per hour and the purchase of pain-killers by the one hundred thousand. All entered in, all data entered, all computed and number crunched. The price of life and the price of pain.

There was a price for keeping John's body. The cost of the wages, the cost of the capital goods, the fridge, the running costs, the cost of depreciation, the cost of administration. There were the costs to come. The coffin, the grave and the transport to the grave. And the administration, the death certificate, the listing of the grave. It all cost. Everything does.

Staff Nurse Lucerne costs money. Thousands and thousands every year and thousands to train her, to teach her what to do. Her blue overall dress costs money and the apron and her gloves and her thermometer. Everything costs money, the dressings, the cream for the bed sores, the time she spends holding Lettie's hands – it costs.

Lucerne smiled. Her high cheeks lifted a little and her light brown skin moved. Her lips parted and her teeth were regular clean white and ordered. Her eyes had dark lashes and her neck faded long into her shoulders. She smiled at the porter. There was something between them.

Yolanda loved the city. You arrived with no history and made your way. Everyone was a no one, an anonymous drop in the sea of people many millions strong. The chaos was a cloak; you owed no one anything and could construct your own part.

She arrived with nothing but a week in a friend's flat. Next, she had work and a room in a shared house and then another job and then Yolanda rented her own flat. And she had a boyfriend and she laughed in London pubs with his friends and with her friends. The beer and the vodka and all sat closely together on bench seats around tables circled with stools, laughter and noise and youthful faces flushed with alcohol and mocking and teasing and the sense of a closeness as they sat happily together with so much before them.

At work, in her office, Yolanda found everyth ng easy. As she had at school, she found no difficulty in achieving what was required. There was no hidden force obstructing her or sabotaging her or destroying what she created. She applied her will and energy and effort and achieved the company's goals and targets. Yolanda delivered.

Her colleagues were women and her clients were mostly women and her staff were all women. She breezed through days and weeks and functioned comfortable in a role that was defined and delineated. Yolanda was always happy to laugh in a bar or a club or at any event. She made money, she was paid well.

One day Jacky phoned the office at eight forty-five. Jacky was Deputy Manager, Yolanda was Manager. They worked together for two or maybe three years. Jacky admired Yolanda, followed her methods, duplicated her style of work and was loyal and good and would never tolerate a bad word against her. Jacky loved it when Yolanda called her 'Jacks' and said, 'Uno Blanco time Jacks,' when they had a wine at the end of the day.

Yolanda knew that Jacky was in bed with her new boyfriend and was phoning in sick with an excuse. Alison held the phone and covered the mouthpiece and said, 'Yolanda – it's Jacky for you.'

Yolanda said, 'Take a message please.'

Alison spoke down the phone, 'Yolanda asked me to take a message.' Jacky was a little taken aback. She did not expect this. She expected Yolanda to take the call and for there to be a conversation about how bad her migraine was and to discuss any outstanding issues regarding Jacky's sales and then for Yolanda to probably say *Take the day off* or maybe to say *Come in lunchtime*. Jacky was Yolanda's top saleswomen – always had been.

She did not expect to have to leave a message with Alison. Jacky was perplexed and panicked, she said, 'Tell Yolanda I'm in hospital. I've got a thrombosis in my leg.'

Alison heard the panic in her voice and said, 'Hold on a minute Jacky, hold on,' and covered the mouthpiece and looked up and Yolanda was looking away but glanced at her and Alison said with whispered concern, 'She's in hospital.'

And Yolanda immediately said, 'Ask her which one.'

Jacky told Alison she was in the Royal College and when Alison put the phone down Yolanda was looking at her. Alison repeated what Jacky had said.

Yolanda stood up and went to the petty cash tin and pulled out a twenty-pound note. She gave it to Alison and said, 'Go to the florists and send some flowers to the hospital.' Yolanda knew that Jacky was lying.

Alan walked away from Sue's door. She had said, 'Hi – what do you want?' and he had stumbled without words quite taken aback by her confidence and careless tone.

He had said, 'Can I come in.'

And when she said so lightly, *No* he had felt a surge of feeling and she carried on, 'No sorry, someone is here,' and Alan felt a rage through him.

Looking at her with desire that had been rising all day he couldn't find anything more than a grunted syllable, a hopeless, 'Oh,' before he turned away.

He wanted her so much, her body had haunted him all day and all day he had been tormented between dozing sleep by flashbacks to the night, to the smell of her, to her breasts in her hands. *No* she had said and the *Someone's here* was a warning, a threat to prevent him from doing anything. It was a way of stopping it.

He walked between the two blocks, past the sad mound with its single swing through the car parking at the entrance to the estate and out onto the road. Cars drove past him. Opposite was the gaggle of tower blocks and left on the corner a modern concrete pub. Left again past the row of cheap food outlets, fried chicken, Chinese, Indian, chips, kebabs and towards the all-night grocery.

In the shop Abdul looked up at Alan, Alan laid on the charm, 'Alright Abdul, give us two cans.'

Abdul put on a gentle smile. 'Sorry but you know I cannot serve alcohol after eleven.' There was no one in the shop. Abdul's cousin was in the stockroom eating.

Alan was sitting on his internal brewed up distress but he was managing it fine when it came to relations with Abdul. Keeping it light he said, 'Abdul, don't be a dick, man, just give me two cans.'

And Abdul knew that the easy tone was a front and that it was not the real Alan and that he had an option here to take the easy road.

'OK I know you – you're a good boy,' said Abdul, and put the two cans of strong lager in a bag. 'But you must be careful now – don't let anyone see you now.'

The shopkeeper was trying to stay co-conspirator.

Alan took the bag smiling broadly. 'Ta Abdul – now get that small vodka for me,' Abdul's heart sank. The boy was taking advantage but he did it anyway, tired of the game, tired of the stress, tired of risking his life to make a living.

Alan took the bag and Abdul entered the figures into the cash register and looked up and asked for, 'Twelve pounds twenty-six.'

Alan smiled. 'You're alright – I'll bring it tomorrow,' and walked out in night where cars drove past and a helicopter moved across the near night sky as planes tracked constantly west towards the busiest airport ever.

John's body lay on the tray in the fridge in the bowels of the hospital. It troubled Derek Gerrard. A loose end to be tied up. Something not right, not processed and something somehow disturbing.

Patient affairs and Pat Driscombe did not want to know. The staff nurse did not want to know and the body was using up space. As he returned to the morgue Derek reflected on the situation. Everything was normal and routine, even the PMs but suddenly something new. Or really just something new to him.

He entered the number combination of the door to the morgue. His desk was there like a sentinel in front of the fridges. Past the desk you could see where the room opened up, L-shaped, to the right. Round that corner was the area for the PMs. Derek Gerrard always called them PMs even to strangers. Hoping he would have to clarify to the uninitiated – post-mortem.

Derek's phone rang and he's said, 'OK, I'm here. Bring them down,' and he opened up his newspaper and settled down to read and wait for his next arrival.

While the fridges hummed and while the morgue porter read about a Hollywood star sniffing cocaine and entertaining prostitutes, the lift clunked down with Ernest Browning, now dead, on the trolley with the two porters and Staff Nurse Lucerne. Lucerne had a wet smudge of tears on her cheeks and a redness around her eyes.

'Oh – it's you again,' said Derek Gerrard to Lucerne when they entered the morgue. 'Better watch out – you'll get a reputation,' he sniggered.

Lucerne set her face hard and got through the paperwork and signed the ledger and stood over the porters to make sure the body was carefully transferred from the trolley to the elevating platform and into the fridge. She set her spirit hard against Gerrard and disregarded his every movement, every word, and saw him diminish before her.

Finally it was done and Lucerne and the two porters were ready to leave. The older man was struggling to open the door and Derek Gerrard said, 'Leave it. Leave it,' urgently and, 'You'll break it,' and moved forward, 'Let me do it.'

As he pushed past the small porter gathered at the door he made sure he pushed out his genitals so that they brushed against the shape of Lucerne's behind. As she recoiled he half giggled under his breath and said, 'Let me through, won't you,' as if she was obstructing him.

Outside the older porter said, 'I'm going for a smoke,' and Lucerne and the younger man went back to the lifts.

'You OK?' he said.

And Lucerne said, 'Yeah, I'm OK — it's just that the crash team laughed — and he was a gem you know. A really nice man.'

They spoke more on the way back to the ward and Lucerne explained that Browning had an embolism and had dropped down dead and she had called the emergency resuscitation team who had looked at his notes and as her recall petered out, she just said, 'Why don't you come round to mine tonight?'

Things were never the same between Jacky and Yolanda. Jacky apologised and tried to explain and delivered the best ever sales figures and stayed late. Yolanda never showed her a moment's tolerance or acceptance or acknowledged their previous friendship. A wall came between them and Yolanda never flinched from her total disregard for the young woman who had lied to her.

With time Jacky became angry, then disillusioned and Yolanda made an excuse and did not go to her leaving party. One day after she had gone Alison asked Yolanda about Jacky and got a dismissive, 'I should have just sacked her.'

And Yolanda laughed and joked with her friends and drank wine and beer in bars and had money and holidays in the sun. A few noticed her hard edges, saw the way she could cut people out but it never seemed to take anything out of her. The city kept people rolling into her life and under the sun and under the moon Yolanda grabbed life and laughed.

Her father, Dr Jones, was scared of the city, of its violence and disorder and its anonymous cloak. There was nowhere organised to park his car and no one knew who he was. On the jumble of public transport, he was a no one and mixed in with the deranged and insane. No one stood aside for him and held him in respect. On the streets of the city he had no rank or status.

In all the chaos of a thousand peoples from a thousand lands jumbled together to feed and make families to build themselves a life, Yolanda swam effortlessly and shared generously everything she achieved. There was laughter in her house and friends entertained with drinks and music and long evenings.

Yolanda had a house and a car and was organised and efficient. Work and money was easy. She could talk all day on the phone. Sometimes she felt like the back of her brain was melting, as if it was shutting down like a shadow engulfing a hillside. But she could pull it back and get back at it, selling and managing and producing great figures. You couldn't see it from the outside. It was a momentary flash of concern and it was gone. Maybe for a few days, maybe for a few weeks, sometimes for months, but it always came back.

Alan walked back to the estate and down the passage behind Sue's house. He could see the downstairs light was on behind closed curtains. He went back and sat on the single swing and opened a can of lager.

Mr Hong Kong walked past quickly. Everyone called him that. He worked in the Chinese take away and spoke hardly any English. Alan spat at the dirt between his feet and rocked slowly on the swing. There was no tenderness now in his thoughts about Sue. That day he had wanted to see her again, to speak with her and to somehow be good to her.

Now she had thrown that back in his face. Closed the door on him and left him out in the cold, discarded like used tissue. She had barred him from her comfortably furnished and carpeted house, barred him from her flesh and left him out under the city sky mocked by an indifferent moon.

Alan was fit and strong. No one gave him any trouble or took advantage of him and yet this lone woman could carelessly snub him. She had taken him in and then put him out and left him bitter at his own soft sweet thoughts. He drank some more.

From where he sat he had a sightline down between the two blocks to Sue's front door. He had finished both cans of alcohol and smoked two tobacco and marijuana cigarettes when her door opened and a buggy was pushed out of the door followed by a dark figure. Alan could just make out the women saying their goodbyes and he got off the swing and moved out of sight.

Natalie walked up past the swing, pushing the buggy and Alan stayed out of sight. He had known Natalie most of his life and knew the father of the boy in the pushchair. He was surprised she was round at Sue's; Natalie was not the sort of girl that Sue mixed with. Natalie's house had a rug, a TV, and a busted settee in the front room. Her bed was a double mattress on the floor.

Alan went back to the swing elated. When Sue said she had someone there he thought it might be a man, or family. It might have been some friends of Will's going round to try to get some sex or some other guy Sue wanted more from. It could have been some man with money or a job or a better talker or a car or loads of cocaine. But it wasn't, it was just Natalie. It wasn't her sister or one of their friends, it wasn't anything unknown, it was just another mum from the estate. It was nothing.

Alan relaxed but then filled immediately with a neediness for Sue. He wanted to see her. She was just there behind that door. He wanted her. He wanted to see her like last night, he wanted to see her like she was then. But he had seen her and she wasn't like that. She was cold and careless and *What do you want* and *No* and *No*.

There was something he wanted, something he needed and it was his way to get it. Take it. Like robbing someone when you had to. Alan did that sometimes. Street robbery. It was easy as long as you picked the right victim. As long as you judged the balance of power right it was easy. Easy to get what you wanted from them.

He went down to Sue's door and knocked. And pressed the bell. He heard her moving about and the hall light came on. He could hear her approaching the door. She said, 'Who's there?'

And Alan said, 'It's me.'

And she said, 'It's too late.'

And he said, 'I want to tell you something.'

And she said, 'Leave it now, Alan.'

He pressed the bell and knocked again a bit more loudly. He raised his voice again, 'Sue,' and the scene was finely balanced. Any upping of the voice level and someone would be disturbed, would see that boy banging on Will's door and see Sue compromised.

Sue was fumbling with the batteries in a white box that powered the doorbell. Alan noticed the bell didn't ring and rapped harder on the door. Sue thought she could cope with him and talk to him and opened the door an inch with a flustered, 'For fuck's sake, Alan calm down,' and he was in. In her house. Thank goodness the kids did not wake up. He walked into the sitting room.

She followed him and he turned round and grabbed her hair at the back of her head and she gasped and was forced onto her knees while all she could feel was the burning roots of her hair being ripped out. He pushed his prick in her face until she took it and then forced her over the couch and fucked her hard from behind. It hurt Sue but she managed to look up when the door to the room began to open and she forced out a desperate, 'Emma, go back to your room now,' and the door opened no further and as Alan breathed hard and grabbed her buttocks she could make out a child's footsteps going up the stairs.

Derek Gerrard liked to go home after work and cook himself something to eat. Then out to the Spread Eagle and drink beer and watch any sport they had on the television. He knew everything that was to know about the Spread Eagle and considered himself to have a senior position in the cohort of patrons known as *The regulars*.

At nine o'clock he was settled in his position on his stool at the bar and Mick the young porter was knocking on the door of Staff Nurse Lucerne with a bottle of wine in his hand. Nurse Lucerne answered the door in a long plain white T-shirt and bare feet. She was happy and confident as she asked him in – pleased that he was there and pleased with the wine and glad that he looked smart and clean and had a gleam in his eye.

'I was going to get changed but thought you know I cannot be bothered and we're not going anywhere and you see me in that awful uniform all day so why.' She chattered happily liking having a man in her flat and getting glasses ready in her tiny kitchen alcove.

Mick sat down on the small two-seater settee and Maria put on music and offered to cook something but he wasn't hungry. She sat on a chair at the small table and drank her wine and they talked. Mick could see her breasts against her T-shirt were large and she wore no bra and her nipples were occasionally prominent. She could see his shape in his clean jeans and his strong arms and narrow waist. They were young, healthy and there was physical attraction in the air as Mick found his eyes drawn to her heavy thighs where the T-shirt hung over them. Maria drank another glass of wine and saw herself in the mirror. She was flushed and smiling and alive and looked great.

And Mick stood up off the settee and she thought he was looking or the bathroom but he took two steps towards her and told her direct to her face, 'Maria – you're gorgeous,' and kissed her and kissed and she pressed herself against him and his hands were on her flesh.

She shuddered with pleasure as he found her nipples and pulled away with her arms behind his neck and said, 'Let's go to bed.'

There were times that Yolanda had felt completely free. When she was a whole continent away and roaming from city to city no one could reach her or know her next move. Then in the big city making her own way at first it felt free. At first it was all her.

They say the moon is one part of the earth thrown into space and held there by unseen forces forever in orbit.

There is some connection but it can be regulated and understood like days in the year and tables with the times of the tides. Unseen though the connection remains.

Dr Jones hated the city but his daughter was never out of touch. He could always reach her, there was the phone and Miranda and Adrian and her mother. All of them were encouraged to visit her. Miranda would turn up at her office with a cake tin, with a cake that she and Gwen had cooked.

Yolanda spoke cheerfully about her family to colleagues and friends and often mentioned them. Her father was a top doctor and they lived a wealthy suburban life. People envied her family envied her father's status and wealth and could see from the phone calls and from the occasional visits they were a close and loving bunch.

Adrian would phone up and say are you going for a drink and tag along and sit in the corner hardly muttering a word before leaving for the train home at a sensible time. And Miranda would appear with something from Mum. She had turned out sort of shabby and frail and timid. Dr Jones would phone.

People were curious and made assumptions and Yolanda rode with them and let the construct fly. Dr Jones was effective on the phone. He had been on a one-day course called business communication for the telephone and had learnt to deal with action points only. He would ring and say, 'Good Morning, can I speak with Yolanda,' and wait and when she came on the line would say, 'We are having lunch for your mother's birthday on the eighteenth. You will be there?' and pause before finishing, 'Good,' and putting down the phone.

Yolanda would ride the train out to the suburbs. The housing would thin out until after six stations the scruffy fields and then further on woodland and lush green pasture between wealthy commuter towns. As arranged, someone would be waiting at the station at an agreed time to pick her up. Mostly it would be Adrian, but sometimes Miranda or her mother.

She would go to the house with them and take part in the activity, to celebrate, the anniversary, the meal to mark this or that occasion and as discussed with Dr Jones, catch the early train in the morning because there was always a reason not to get the last train. It wouldn't be fair for someone not to be able to have a glass of wine or this person was not on the car insurance or something.

Sometimes her mother would greet her with some affection but would soon comment on something, her appearance, her weight, her hair with a tangible dissatisfaction that was almost a sneer. Gwen would be sat at the table, her body present, her attempts at conversation hopeless and mocked and just not too drunk. Dr Jones kept the evening on schedule.

Then it would be night and in the morning on the train Yolanda longed for her desk and her phone and work and colleagues and the all-enveloping warm anonymty of the city where she could live another day, another day. Friends asked about her evening and she would say, 'Oh you know, it was fine,' and move the conversation on.

Alan was smoking weed and telling Sue about his greatest ever jobs. He called a criminal enterprise a job. Sue had known boys like this all her life and she could see he was going nowhere in his lawless career. She had known boys his age who were retailing thousands of pounds of drugs per week. Alan was scumming along on the bottom rung. He would go to prison. In his bragging he mentioned violence against individuals with excitement and indifference.

Sue was tired, exhausted and struggling to plot her way out of the situation. Sue blamed herself for it. It was her fault for starting this thing and now Alan was punctuating his drawling tones with, 'You know what I mean, babes?' and 'The thing is, babes,' the term of affection was also a sign of proprietorship and ownership. As Sue was fighting off sleep, she was hearing him say 'You'll be alright with me, babes, we'll be fine,' as he rumbled on.

In the morning, in a few hours, in three hours' time the girls would be up and need breakfast and taking to school and Alan was saying, 'I'll have to crash here,' and she didn't want the girls to see him and why couldn't he just go now.

He said he would be alright on the settee and Sue said, 'Listen Alan, go home now and we can have some proper time tomorrow – you know I'll make it up to you,' and she squeezed him and got him out of the house and fell instantly asleep on the bed.

The sun rose and battered the concrete at the heart of the city with the first blasts of heat and Sue sat up with a start as Sharon crawled under the bed sheet next to her and said, 'We are definitely going to be late today,' as the child snuggled up to her mother wanting warmth, security, safety, love and affection. It was nine o'clock. They were late for the second day running.

At nine-thirty am Sharon timidly went into her classroom. Miss Brooks greeted her with delight and tried to overcome the girl's obvious sense of shame. Sharon knew that it was wrong to be late and she knew she and Emma were not the sort of girls who were late or didn't have nice shoes. Self-consciously Sharon sat at her table. Miss Brooks glanced out the window and could see Sue walking away and a flush of anger shot through the young teacher. And concern. That day she kept her eye on Sharon and gave her little tasks to do but she could see the young girl was distracted and ill at ease.

Sue walked down the hill towards the estate smoking a cigarette. She was unwashed. She didn't know where to go. If she went to her house Alan would be knocking on her door. The sun was blazing down. Cars were going past and an ambulance siren was moving down the parallel road. Her feet were falling flat on the pavement and the stone was reverberating up her legs. She was tired. An unforgiving city was stretching for many miles in all directions. She pulled the toxic fumes from the cigarette into her lungs. It was if Will was dead and had been for years. She had nowhere to go.

Derek Gerrard finished his last pint of beer and walked back to his flat in the block across the road. Inside he took off his clothes, dropped them on the bedroom floor and flopped on the bed. He turned out the bedside light after fumbling for the snooze button to turn on the radio that was also on the bedside table. For five minutes a talk radio phone-in entered his consciousness before he was asleep in sheets that had not been changed for a fortnight.

Maria Lucerne woke up and saw Mick's back upright as he sat on the side of the bed recovering his clothes.

'You running off,' she teased lightly.

'No, I've work, I can't not,' he stumbled.

'No worries,' said Lucerne. 'Did you have a good time?'

'Sure, yes Maria, you're gorgeous,' he said, and there was an unspoken *but* at the end of his sentence.

Lucerne half sat up – pulling the sheet over her breasts. She was smiling and easy. 'Mick, it's OK. I know this is just one of these things. You haven't broken my heart.'

A grimace passed Mick's face. One of those things and an unbroken heart was touched with failure, a familiar sort of rejection. But it passed as soon as he stood up and was ready to walk away, to go out into another day.

Maria gestured him to her and he lent down and she hugged him and then the door closed behind him and he was gone and she snuggled under the covers a satisfying physical shroud over her. The night had been long. He had the vigour of youth and had matched her need. As the day gathered strength Lucerne slept on.

Next time she woke it was to prepare for the late shift and she was into the routine of eating, and ironing clothes, and putting washing in the machine. The radio played and she looked at herself in the mirror and thought of the pleasure she had taken and almost laughed as she pushed up her breasts but the small apartment suddenly rushed her with a belt of loneliness.

Out on the streets, in the queue for public transport she felt unknown and unwanted and without trace in the city, where she had found no love. The passing comfort had fixed nothing and under a sky of luminous grey standing beside a channel of heaving traffic Lucerne steadied herself with thoughts of work and the mundane. She cursed the intimacy of the night with a rationale and took the indifference of the day.

In the tumble of arms and legs and bursting lust there had been no love. Just that moment but nothing beyond. The bus pulled up. Staff Nurse Lucerne went to work.

The office was busy. Yolanda was the best performing manager in the group. The phone rang and her staff worked hard and posted great figures. It was sales. Some couldn't take the pressure and left. She rose quickly and made her name and got paid good bonuses. Yolanda did well and her staff did well.

One day Geoff asked her about a bruise on her leg. She looked down. There were two bruises one below and one above her knee. 'I don't know what that is,' she said, 'I always bruise easily.' Geoff did not want to seam possessive or intrusive so it was not mentioned again. Friends came round and drank wine and they laughed together.

One day at work the thing in her brain started. She was in the toilet. She stood up and her breath went and she gasped as if someone was crushing her chest and she gulped again and it was fine and she went outside the toilet and the rushing of blood through her head stopped and she was fine.

Days followed days and seasons and years and holidays and parties and she got comfortable with Geoff in the flat, her friend George, the gay guy from Greece, was sat opposite her at her desk as the business day closed and he saw her freeze for a moment and said, 'Hey, you OK?' and he could see that for a moment she wasn't. She reassured him and George said, 'You want to watch out – stress, panic attacks and all that in your job, darling, pressure I expect.'

Watching soap operas at home Yolanda could relax and she found out more about the stress and the panic attacks and stopped drinking coffee and noticed how much she drank. She wanted to solve it, to beat it to carry on day after day to take every day of life.

Somehow the fixes never quite wiped out the sudden creeping sensation, the feeling of the brain closing, the sudden refocus that required every atom of will to hold it off, to push it away to get back into the moment. At yoga classes she breathed, her cupboards were full of the healthiest foods and her body was fit and healthy and strong.

Yolanda had days on the beach and stood on mountain tops and sailed boats and rode horses and walked many miles and cycled and laughed with friends and slept at night. Geoff was there, her friends were there, her work was there, her bank accounts were in credit.

She suggested to Geoff that they should get rid of the phone in the flat. He asked her why and she said it was just a suggestion and it was not spoken of again. There were carefree holidays to the Mediterranean, swimming on the beach and drinking and dancing at night. These days of bliss and youth and bright summer days camping by the river that ran off the mountains and a small boat sailing along the coast and all-night parties in houses with friends and strangers and the smell of cigarettes and beer and music rocking the walls. The jokes friends made about each other and the circle of care that was them.

You cannot hold joy or count the days of untroubled fun or remember all the laughter that went on and on. Years are numbers but the moments of happiness are gone like snowflakes, like the stars that you stared at one night in the high sky are not here after dawn, like seasons happiness comes and is gone.

Debbie phoned Yolanda and said 'You'll never guess what,' and Yolanda had no clue what Debbie was going to say or any idea what was coming, of what her friend of two years was telling her, 'I'm having a baby.'

Sue couldn't face her sister or anyone. She couldn't go home where Alan would be watching out for her. She walked listlessly to Natalie's and was pleased she was there and pleased to see her and inviting her in with a commentary of diverting woes regarding furniture and some proposed redecoration. Sue sat down on the battered settee.

Natalie made tea. Sue looked around the room at the faded curtains that did not fit and the scratched and peeling wallpaper, at the dirty rug on the floor and at the old TV set standing on a wobbly old table. There were three unframed photos on the mantelpiece and an old vase with two peacock feathers in it. The pushchair was in the corner, there was no carpet in the hallway or on the stairs. A line of grime, accumulated hand marks and scuffs scarred all the walls.

In the kitchen Natalie boiled the kettle delighted to see Sue and delighted she had both tea and fresh milk. Her fridge had chips off the white enamel but worked. There was cheap women's underwear drying on a rack in the corner. Natalie had washed it by hand. In a washing basket there was a collection of children's clothes, tracksuits and T-shirts. Natalie was wearing a T-shirt and leggings and flip-flop shoes.

She asked Sue, 'Do you want sugar?' and quickly added some to her guest's drink from paper sachets taken from a burger bar. She gave Sue the cup, the only one without a chip out of it, and sat down on a kitchen chair opposite the settee.

Sue pulled out her pack of cigarettes and asked, 'Do you want one?

'No, I'm giving up,' said Natalie.

'Oh go on,' said Sue, and she knew that Natalie had no money until her benefit cheque arrived. They talked and smoked another cigarette and somehow no mention was made of Alan or Sue's situation or Will.

'This is lovely,' said Sue after a while, and Natalie was warmed by her new friendship and Sue stood up and asked her, 'Do you want to come over to mine tonight?' and Natalie said, 'Oh yeah that would be great.'

'Good,' said Sue, 'Bring your little monster and we can talk more then – I might even buy a bottle.'

Natalie laughed, delighted at the invite and also by the suggestion that there was more to be said, more to be shared between the women.

Sue said, 'Bye, see you later.' Natalie let her out and Sue could see at some point Natalie's front door had been attacked. The outer skin of plywood was caved in a foot above the pavement and scratched and dented around chest height. The lock had been replaced but the paintwork had not been made good where the repair had been done. As she walked away, she glanced back at the scruffy dwelling and was pleased that Natalie was coming to hers that evening.

The city droned on with the day. Aircraft crossed the sky and buses carried people-loads towards the lines of retail outlets. On the estate a single magpie stood on the fence at the back of Sue's house and the shone sun down on a windless day. Indoors Sue tried to reorder the mess, emptying ashtrays and gathering up clothes and putting dishes and crockery by the sink. Then she sat down for a moment and leant back on the couch and unguarded was caught by sleep.

Outside, just past the green with its single swing, two women with young preschool children in pushchairs stood talking. There was concern in their voices and they glanced back towards Sue's. They parted and the postman appeared pushing his red cart and an old man walked off the estate towards the shops wearing slippers and carrying an old shopping bag. In the moment of quiet there was a loud human squawking and looking up you could see a woman on a tenth-floor balcony of the white tower block crying and struggling as an unseen man threatened to throw her over. Then she was gone and a woman walked past with a child's pushchair hung with a plastic bag full of sugar drinks, pizza and packs of sweet treats.

A youth swaggered behind his fighting dog in its studded harness and Wayne O'Connell walked past with a stolen laptop in his sports bag. Sue slept on and the school day ended and the classrooms emptied and the children whose carers were late had to sit in the hall quietly waiting. Emma sat next to her sister. This had never happened to them before.

Derek Gerrard reviewed the large ledger on his desk. There were names and hospitals numbers and signatures.

Slowly bodies worked through the system from the ward to the fridge to the undertaker in most cases. Some had a PM, and some had special religious requirements. For some deceased the time spent under the care of Derek Gerrard was weeks and for others just days.

The phone rang. You had to have an appointment to bring in a deceased. It had to be arranged. When it came to the final procedures at the end of the line, at the point post terminal, at the point at which a medic signed a certificate saying *dead* Derek Gerrard became a key player and man of power. He took the call and disguised his pleasure in being needed.

He made a note on a yellow stick-it pad and went back to his ledger and his fat finger scanned down the entries pausing and crossing the page occasionally. His finger passed over John, hesitating but not stopping and completed its journey down to the latest name that had been added. Everything and everyone was in order, bar one, bar the one called John, the unknown, unclaimed, unwanted body.

The phone rang again and he adopted a jaded and difficult tone before he had heard a word.

'I've already got one coming down this morning and as you know we do things properly here... I'm not cutting any corners,' and he listened before interjecting, 'Yes, well everyone is busy but I don't see how I can do it before my lunch.'

He listened to the voice on the phone before offering, 'When are you finishing?' and now controlling the situation, 'OK – I'll tell you what – bring them down at half past – alright – and I'll get them in the book and you can get off pronto,' and the voice was grateful and Derek was generous, 'No problem, no problem – I'll sort it,' as he settled his flab back into the chair.

His eye caught the entry for John and he thought briefly of going back up to see Pat Driscombe about it but instead pulled out a catalogue of electrical goods to leaf through while he waited for the new deceased to appear with its escort.

The hospital ground on with its appointments and processing of the populace. Cars and taxis and ambulances, and motorbike couriers carrying blood and organs, drove up to the doors and the building stood high and white and ten floors large, a block against and across a portion of the sky. Babies were born and bacteria ate into flesh and surgeons opened human bodies to the air and tubes drained pus from rotting intestines and then was a whole floor of madness and another of old age and bodies crumbling to death.

Staff Nurse Lucerne was having a handover meeting. As soon as she saw the agency nurse, the temporary cover, get up to say hello she knew things were not right. The woman did not greet her with anything other than a desperate relief.

'So what's been happening?' said Lucerne.

'Oh – well Mrs Johnson had another stroke last night

and went this morning – and Tom Parfitt dropped dead as I was doing the drugs trolley.'

Lucerne rocked back on her chair. Her colleague continued, 'I called the crash team – but when they got here they...' she hesitated, she knew Lucerne was fond of the upright and almost sprightly old man.

'What?' said Lucerne. 'What did they do?'

'Well they saw his notes.'

'And?' said Lucerne...

'They didn't do anything – um – they laughed.'

Lucerne looked at the woman. Her badge said her name was Fondant. She was a temporary nurse booked for the week and probably hoping to work anywhere else but on the geriatric ward where this man Parfitt was walking around with an enormous clot of blood in his heart, which would at some random moment break loose and send him a breathless quick death. Lucerne's flush of grief was an anger at the emergency resuscitation teams' lack of respect.

She just sighed and Fondant went on, 'and Mrs Johnson never woke up properly and I got Dr Azim? And she was gone.'

So Lettie was gone too. And Lucerne could hardly move. She didn't like the *Didn't wake up properly*. What did that mean? Lettie had been fine and did she wake up or not this morning?

Fondant carried on, 'Azim certified them. They are both laid out and I found the shrouds... eventually.'

Fondant was looking at Lucerne. Preparing her two deceased, washing them, stuffing their orifices, brushing their hair was hard work. Lucerne acknowledged it.

'Oh good.'

'I've spoken to the morgue, we can take them down.'

'Great,' said Lucerne emptily.

Yolanda began to see small children and babies everywhere. They went in buggies all over the city, at every shop, at every bus stop. She began to see pregnant women and the baby stuff in the chemists and the family pages of the newspapers and the baby care magazines. She found herself watching women holding their babies and noting their equipment, the special bags with the nappies, the different styles of baby buggy.

The train rocked her back to the suburban station and she wanted to see what her mother had used. She dug out the photo albums and looked at pictures of Gwen holding babies. Her mother stared blankly at the camera with the bundles of white clothes in her arms, her face lifeless. Except for the pictures with Richard in. When her husband was there, Gwen was alive. There was one where she was looking up at him totally absorbed by the man. Yolanda shuddered.

At the evening meal Yolanda asked her mother a strange question about what drugs they gave her when she was having babies and Gwen flustered with Martinis and wine dismissed her. 'Oh for goodness sake, I don't know — it was a very long time ago.'

And Richard Jones interjected, 'Your Mother only ever refused an epidural on each occasion,' with his medical authority.

As the meal finished Richard Jones said, 'I am going to telephone Geoff this week. I have booked a villa and am going to invite you. I will give him the details,' and in the morning on the train going back to the city Yolanda sat solid and heavy in her seat. A weight sat on her, a weight of something past hurt, past anger, a weight of the inevitable, of a certain despair.

In the office Liz approached her smiling with a freshly printed paper. She put it on Yolanda's desk, 'Top ten, champagne with Alec on Thursday.' Her eyes were sparkling, a grin on her lips.

Yolanda felt the blood rushing at the base of her skull and it beginning to spread up her head and she wanted the woman gone and she said heavily, 'Good I want everyone cold calling all morning,' and waited without moving for Liz to leave her and to tell the team that they were expected to spend the morning in the most difficult, tiresome and fruitless task they had.

The family holiday with Adrian and Miranda and Geoff was in a large Mediterranean villa with a pool where Yolanda swam every morning, early before any others got up, before Geoff. Gwen was kept drunk every day and every evening Dr Jones booked a restaurant and they all ate together. And every morning Yolanda was down at the pool.

Then back in the city and Geoff was quite useless and there were children everywhere and Debbie with her round swollen tummy and telling her, 'Look – put your hand here,' and feeling the movement and wanting it but the blood pounding in her brain, over her skull, down to her brow, past her hairline, coming into her eyes, pounding.

Breathe and it's gone but tired and drained, and people saying, 'How are you?' and 'Good Holiday?' and him on the phone saying next week 'We are going to…' and no peace from it ever, as if it was never going to stop and always came back and it was gone, and breathe, and it was nothing. What was it? What was it that would not ever leave her alone?

No one knew. No one could see it. Lying down on the couch, a candle burning and quiet music to meditate to and no one there and the peace of the universe and it eased and the night wore on and the morning came and the sun rose over the city and the woman that was Yolanda breathed in another day.

Sue woke up as her front door was being battered She was sweating. On her feet disorientated the banging of her door continued. She had taken the battery out of the bell. She went to the door. It was Natalie with Emma and Sharon.

Natalie was grinning, 'I hope you had a good sleep,' she said, ushering the two young girls into their mother's house, 'I'll see you later.'

'Yeah of course,' said Sue gratefully taking her daughters in.

Sue sat the girls down in front of the television and put on her shoes and went out to the shop on the road that ran down the side of the estate. She bought pre-cooked meals that just needed heating up and a bottle of wine and cigarettes and carbonated sugar drinks for the girls.

Back indoors the children were quiet and absorbed by the moving images and Sue put their food in the oven to heat up and poured herself a glass of wine. She had three sips and then it was half gone. The children ate their food on the settee and she said, 'You two are having an early night tonight.'

Natalie came to the door at eight-thirty with Wayne asleep in the pushchair. Sharon and Emma were already in bed and there was just enough wine left for a glass each.

Natalie had put on a bright yellow blouse over a clean pair of leggings and changed her flip-flops for a pair of shiny black shoes with heels. Sue was unchanged and unwashed. The plates the children had eaten off were stacked on the kitchen worktop and there was a full bag of rubbish in the corner.

Sue was feeling better, 'Oh I look such a mess.'

Natalie rebuffed her with, 'Come off it, Sue, you're brilliant looking. I wish I had a figure like yours,' and Sue went to the cupboard and took out another twenty pounds and said, 'If you pop around to the shop and get another bottle of wine, I'll jump in the shower,' and Natalie went out into the evening air taking Sue's keys so she could let herself back into the house.

Sue stood naked in the bath and set the shower head attachment on its hook on the wall and let the warm water spray over her head and shoulders. She leaned forward and let it beat down on her back and then shampooed her hair until suds ran down all over her body. Sue turned her face up into the water and let it rinse off her hairline and pour down her face. Water ran off her face and head and off her shoulders and she picked up a bar of soap and rubbed it under each arm and washed off the foam by raising her arms, so the shower could spray it away. She let all the soap and shampoo run down her body over her belly and down her thighs. She took the soap and washed between her legs and between her buttocks. She put her foot up on the side of the bath and washed her feet, her toes and her calves.

Natalie walked between the blocks of maisonettes in

her high heels and bright blouse for once unencumbered by a child's pushchair or by anything. In her hand she clenched enough money for wine and cigarettes and she was out for the evening, away from her own place. In the shop she bought two bottles of the wine that Sue liked and a small packet of ten cigarettes. She walked down the road and turned down the ramp back to the estate.

Alan and Tony and Ben were at the bottom of the ramp. Tony was sat on the wall and the other two young men were standing. They had just met up and Tony was making a marijuana cigarette. All three watched Natalie approach. 'Where's the party, Nats?' said Ben when she was a few feet away.

'No party – I'm just having a drink at Sue's.' Natalie continued on and just cast her gaze for a spilt second in the direction of Alan, before she was past them and moving quickly towards Sue's front door.

Natalie let herself in and Sue got out of the shower. They had another glass of wine and Natalie told her friend about the brief encounter with them. There was a knock on the door, a polite banging on the wood.

Sue opened the door with Natalie standing behind her. It was Ben who had been nominated to make the approach and was wondering if they wanted some company and a bit of a *chill out* as they, Alan and Tony and Ben, had been thinking of going out to a club but had thought, 'Why spend all that money?' when they could hang out and have a good time around here.

Sue said, 'I don't think so.'

And Natalie laughed, 'You must be joking.'

But Ben allowed them their rejection before pushing a, 'No it will be cool, we'll bring some tunes and a drink.'

And Sue knew that Natalie was quite thrilled at the idea and some part of her wanted more company and felt that with others here Alan would be OK and doubts ebbed as Natalie looked at her, looked up to her and Sue wanted to please her and said lightly, 'OK then.'

Ben went away and came back and Tony and Alan had changed and put clean shirts on and they put a bottle of vodka and two bottles of wine in the kitchen and Alan had been copiously polite and unassuming with Sue as if nothing had happened between them. And Natalie soon stood in the living room with a glass of vodka in her hand, a spliff in the other, a wide smile on her face and shifting her weight from foot to foot, beginning to dance, while Tony opposite her was nodding and laughing saying, 'Come on, Nats, let your hair down.'

Sue was feeling the alcohol and taken a drag or two on a spliff and Alan was telling her she was, 'Easily the best looking woman on the estate,' and that, 'Everyone thought she was hot,' and that he really thought she could be, 'A model.'

Then there was a pause when Wayne started crying in his pushchair and Natalie and Sue had a quick motherly conference and Natalie picked him up and took him upstairs and Sue followed with the pushchair and they put him in the girls' room. Sharon woke up for a moment and Sue said firmly, 'Sshh just go back to sleep, we're just playing music,' and the two women felt they had paid diligence to their children and went downstairs and filled their glasses with alcohol and smoked marijuana and danced together a little and then Tony danced a bit with Natalie and Alan smooched with Sue and Ben sat down heavily in a chair, drunk.

In the lift was Fondant, a porter, and in the special trolley the body of Tom Parfitt. Lucerne did not know Fondant and did not know the porter. She knew Tom Parfitt. He was a big man, over six foot tall and broad shouldered and still big in his old age. Parfitt would get up and sit beside his bed before breakfast and tour the ward making conversation with patients and generally making remarks to nurses. He laughed with Lucerne, 'Watch out here comes the boss,' a 'Don't you worry, I'm still here,' and carried a relentless cheerfulness unbroken by serious looking young doctors waiting to show him X-rays and discuss treatment.

'Thank you, Doc, thank you,' he would say and, 'Don't you worry I know you've done everything you can.'

Lucerne found herself drawn to him every single shift – looking forward to seeing him, looking forward to the immediate warmth of his greeting, 'Here comes beautiful,' to the openness of his laugh. On late shifts she sat with him and asked about his wife. He had been a widower for twenty years.

One night Lucerne asked him about the old hospital and somehow it triggered something in him and he explained, 'After the carry on I had in the war nothing's been the same,' and Lucerne wondered what the *carry on* was and wondered if anyone else knew and if one day she might ask him.

The lift bumped to its stop in the sub-basement and the porter and Fondant manoeuvred the trolley out and down the narrow corridor. They halted at the outer double doors outside the morgue. Lucerne opened the first door and pressed the buzzer on the inner doors. She knew that

Derek Gerhard was expecting them and she knew that he would move reluctantly, slowly, ponderously, insolently about, as they waited.

One night Lucerne sat in the chair beside Tom Parfitt's bed and just said, 'So what was this *carry on* you had in the war, Tom?'

And he laughed lightly and said, 'Oh you don't want to know about that... it was a very blooming long time ago – another world.'

And Lucerne looked at him and saw a glint in his eye and a touch of energy in his voice and pushed on, 'No... go on – what did you do?'

And he turned and faced her propped up on the pillows and looked at her and looked almost young and strong again when he said, 'I was a parachutist.'

'Where did you go?' asked Lucerne.

And he looked at her to make sure she really wanted to know and he said quietly. 'I was in North Africa, I was in Normandy and I was in Holland.'

Derek Gerrard's fat fingers released the lock and a grin showed across his face as the door opened and he saw Lucerne and Fondant. 'Come in, Ladies,' he said. 'What have you got for me today.'

Lucerne had said to Tom Parfitt you must have some stories to tell and the old man laughed. 'Nothing a beautiful young thing like you needs to know, nothing...'

'Oh, come on,' said Lucerne. 'Tell me something I can tell people. Come on,' and she saw in the old man's face a vitality and a pride.

He said, 'Well here's one for you. You know we were Rot Tifoli – red devils – and we had these little lightweight guns, sten guns and they couldn't take a bayonet – so we carried our fighting knives strapped here – on our legs.'

Lucerne listened on. 'So before we were dropped the German general issued an order saying any of us captured with the knife were to be killed... with it. The knife. You see when we got back my mate didn't make it so me and another fella went to his house. His mother chased us down the road. She couldn't bear to see us alive when her son was, you know.'

Parfitt looked at Lucerne. He looked at her very closely. He could see her listening.

Derek Gerrard pulled the trolley into the morgue and looked at the number on Parfitt's wristband and checked it against the entry in his ledger and looked at Lucerne and then looked at Fondant and said, 'Oh yeah I heard about this one – some goon called the crash team.'

Fondant started but Lucerne looked at her and then looked at Derek Gerrard and told him, 'Just do your job.'

Under a night sky framed by the soft round mountains in a valley with a river running through a campsite and away from the fire Yolanda looks up at the stars stretching an infinity of infinities away bright against black. Then one bursts across the sky leaving a trail almost gone before it's seen. A star exploding in the universe and gone before it's seen on earth. If you saw it. Was it even ever there?

Back to the fire and a circle of friends and mugs of late-night coffee laced with cheap brandy and laughter and no one had seen it, no one was looking and there was nothing now left to see. It was gone in darkness and gone in time and the next day Yolanda climbed a mountain and the wind blew in her hair and the clouds touched the hill tops and rain washed the air until the sun broke through and you could see a thousand happy lives in the farms and the village dwellings below.

Another day and back in the city and the streets full of mad people muttering and in the quiet of her flat, the stillness to quell the chaos of the blood rushing through the brain and him saying, 'Of course they have mental health issues,' about this person and about that person and trying to place where this sour breath was that was a memory so close to your face when, when was it, and that relief and despair when it was gone. Hopeless to fight it off as the weight came back, the breath came back and the movement down. Down there. Lips close to your face and you know those teeth.

Breathe and breathe again and steady and it will always come back. In your face and then pushing it away and standing by the window. Opening the window from the second floor and the drop to the paving stones and walking away and bile rising and breakfast wrapped in soft saliva jumping across three feet and hitting the sink. Gagging and gagging and quicker than that star a half taste of something pushed in your mouth gone.

Breathing and breathing and washing away the putrid toast and bile and saliva and pushing away the lumps down the plug and what was it. And another heave and gag of bile and flecks of half-eaten bread in the sink.

It wasn't. It was not. It could not have been. And breathe and breathe. Shuddering and quickening and the drone of the traffic and the aircraft flying over the city while the last remnants are cleaned from the sink and shutting the window and moving on.

Moving on and keeping the window shut and more

days and more life and away from that impulse that would finish all this in a single muscle push like the bodies that flew in front of trains. Just oblivion. But no. Yolanda sat down, a tissue in her hand. Pale faced and exhaustion dug in the lines around her eyes and mouth. Unfocused, gazing across the room her eyelids heavy and unbalanced. Her hands tensed and untensed around a tissue.

Her stomach juddered and oiliness haunted her mouth. She drew her legs up over the chair and pulled an eiderdown over her. Yolanda sat still and breathed in the world and sat unmoved and let everything rest and let her heart pump and blood flow and let her mind stay still, shut like a window.

Natalie sat in one of the two armchairs in Sue's living room. Tony quickly sat on the arm of the chair saying, 'Come on Nats, what is it?'

And Natalie told him, 'I need a rest.'

And Tony leaned forward and gently kissed her neck and said very quietly, 'Come on Nats, have a bit of fun,' and his right hand undid the top two buttons on her blouse as he nuzzled at her neck.

Ben was unconscious in the other chair and Sue was with Alan in the kitchen. Alan pulled Sue against him with his arm around her waist. Sue was too drunk. She swayed against him head flopping unto his shoulder and then she pulled away her head looping backwards her eyes trying to focus on his face. She struggled with the alcohol, with staying conscious against a tide of booze and marijuana and fatigue and sleeplessness.

Alan pulled her against him and pushed at her with his

groin. He rubbed his clothed genitals onto her but felt nothing back. He squeezed her buttock hard with his right hand and put his thigh between her legs. She rocked forward her head rolling onto his shoulder, her arms flapping at her sides. Alan leant back against the kitchen cupboard and put his hand inside Sue's T-shirt and felt her breasts. He pulled at her bra and squeezed at her nipple. Sue put an arm around his neck.

Natalie was giggling as Tony nipped her neck and stroked her breasts and murmured, 'Oh Nats – they're lovely,' and he got his hand inside the washed-out grey bra and felt the weight of her breasts and rolled the nipple between thumb and finger. And Natalie sighed and bathed in the warmth of the attention and then leant forward, and had to sit up and undid her bra behind her back and took it off by pulling first one strap, then the other, down over her hands so her breasts were free beneath her blouse. Tony nuzzled back at her neck and played with her breasts and Natalie stroked his thigh and up towards his prick.

Sue was leaning against Alan using him to keep on her feet. He began to move and taking her with him, still hanging on around his neck, went into the other room and gently dropped her on the settee. Briefly Sue rested her head but Alan filled her mouth with his tongue and pressed her back onto the settee and let his hands roam over her body stroking her sides and thighs.

Natalie saw Alan and Sue come into the room, she saw Alan kissing her on the couch and felt Tony's hand thrusting inside the waistband of her leggings, his fingers slipping inside her knickers and pushing down through her. She eased back in the chair and opened her legs and Tony sighed as she acquiesced and allowed him. In a moment she raised herself off the chair and between them they pulled off her leggings and underwear and Tony was feeling her, licking her nipples.

Outside the night air was warm and the tallest buildings held up red lights into the night sky and police helicopters supervised the movements on the streets below where men moved miniscule between massive concrete lumps. Cars, buses, vans and lorries threaded red and white lights over elevated sections and down the city hub where people drank and danced and took lovers home. Out from the core the lights thinned, there were less cars and less light and most windows were dark behind which all those millions slept. Here, among this endless sprawl every week murder was done. Everyday a child lay neglected and another kilo of heroin was bought or sold.

From Sue's house the first whore house was only four hundred metres and called High Society Sauna. The girls in there were from Europe. There was another one called Daisy's Massage and the girls in there were from the Far East. All over the city they were there, seven days a week. And high on the twenty-second floor, Waheed and Vera were limping along to trade the thirty pounds they had for some rocks and some brown and sit on the settee jabbering nonsense and going unconscious in a small world of filth, of used needles, of blood up the wall, of burnt foil, cigarettes, used condoms and in the kitchen a bin bag bursting with dirty nappies.

Tony had Natalie on the floor and her hand was on his back as he lay on top of her, his jeans down around his knees. She grunted and giggled with a small satisfaction as he entered her and he kept on kissing her neck as Natalie opened her legs wider to get most or more of him in her.

Across the room Alan was pulling off Sue's top and pulling down her jeans and pulling off her knickers as she fought for consciousness against waves of alcohol, against more alcohol and marijuana, against a fatigue and a loss and a lostness. Alan was on his knees on the settee and pushing his dick into her and staying upright as he pushed into her. He looked down at her with one hand at the back of the furniture and the other playing with her breasts and he could look down and see his prick going into her.

And he could see Tony hugged up over Natalie, his head on her neck, and his buttocks rising and dipping down and he could see Natalie's large white breasts and sagging flesh around her belly and her big round breasts with Tony's hands on them and pulling at them. Ben slept on in the chair, and on the estate you could hear a thousand televisions and always somewhere a child crying in the night.

Derek Gerrard looked at Lucerne as he manoeuvred the trolley with the sliding tray elevator mechanism next to the trolley that Tom Parfitt lay on, that the nurses had brought the big deceased soldier down to the morgue on. The trolleys clashed together and Derek Gerrard leaned over the empty trolley and grasped the shroud that Parfitt was in. He grasped a handful of the white material in his left hand and a handful in his right hand. One hand was by Parfitt's hips, the other by his shoulder. Derek Gerrard rocked back pulling the material tight, taking the strain. Then he yanked and the body jerked off one trolley onto the other. The head lolled to rest.

Derek Gerrard looked at the nurses.

'Don't worry I'll do my job,' he said, and spun the trolley with the corpse towards the bank of fridges so that Parfitt would go in head first. The morgue porter opened a door to one of the compartments.

Lucerne remembered the last time she sat down with Parfitt. 'No more war stories for you,' he had said.

'Oh why not?' asked the nurse with a disappointment that perhaps their conversation would be limited.

'You don't want to hear an old man's ramblings do you?' and Parfitt's eyes no longer held the pride and excitement. Instead, there had been a tiredness.

'No, you weren't rambling.' Lucerne could see change in him. 'I was curious, to know what it was like.' She felt she owed him an excuse.

Now Parfitt had looked her hard in the eye. It was a different look. Still with no smile. A certainty and a knowledge was there. The tone was suddenly quite changed. He said, 'You want to know what it was like?'

'Yes,' said Lucerne.

There was silence and a tension and Parfitt's face was fixed and unmoving and his eyes fixed on hers but without a hint of compromise, with a look that reached a long way back, with blue eyes that showed no give, no mercy. You could see no mercy. 'It was butchery,' he said.

And Derek Gerrard slid the old soldier into the fridge deliberately slamming the metal tray and the metal door and the metal trolley. He put the body into the cold air to stop the rot and putrification and he turned to Lucerne and said, 'I'll do my job. Now you do yours.'

Lucerne looked at him and didn't move and Gerrard slowly went back to his desk. Fondant touched her colleague's arm. She wanted to get away and they still had more to do.

Lucerne turned and as she headed for the door Gerrard said, 'See you soon,' and the two nurses set off to bring down the body of Lettie.

If you can shut the window, you can open it and if you do not plunge into oblivion, it only takes a second, the wind of memory may blast you with a thousand visions cascading behind your eyes. Remember that star that is gone and any night you can see the rest of the universe but not that one that shot across the sky and trailing a glowing tail was gone completely. Yes, the one you saw, the one that was here real and gone. All the rest are there and blazing in a thousand histories with names you can recall.

You can see the picnics on the beach and car trips to a foreign country and school plays and things that you saw on the news and sitting here all together watching films and programmes on the television. You remember Christmas and birthdays and grandparents and swimming in the sea. School and teachers and kids at school. Playgrounds and games and friends. Yolanda could remember it.

The window is open and you have to look down and view the reality of that hard paved impact and the breeze blows in a taste of fear of something that might have been. How can you say that you think that at bedtime, that at bedtime… all those childish thoughts were slaughtered by a knowing that it would not last and pray for a change that would stop it. A change in him, in you, in the way that the heavens overlooked uncaring. And how it would never stop. Never. And how you cannot speak.

Yolanda thought of her teacher, of Mrs Rolls who was pleased to see her. Mrs Rolls loved her enthusiasm and desire to please and her hard work. There was warmth and love and afterschool lessons. And hope that somehow Mrs Rolls could get it to stop. Then that day when Yolanda went home and she was there with Richard Jones laughing in his kitchen.

There were all the joys of school and all the joys of those days under the blue suburban sky. But the window was open and Yolanda could not remember when it did not happen. It was always there. Orion or the North Star were in the night sky and he was always there. She, Yo anda, was always there but could not recall the beginning or the end.

Yolanda could shut the window and carry on, carry on working. Carry on paying the bills and taking the train home to the suburban house and sitting with these people and carry on back to life in the great city. But sometimes Yolanda could not stop from wanting to look at the fall, the tumble down and the call of certain peace that would last forever in a thousand caverns of eternity.

Yolanda lay down on the couch. Was it so that these things were even possible. Was it madness? The traffic went past. Buses took people home, lorries carried goods into the city shops. The sun rose and sank and night came and was it coming down to crush her, to make Yolanda another mad woman muttering as she walked the streets. Those things that were like memory could be madness, could be derangement and chemical imbalance and as he said, *Mental health issues* and, *Having a nervous breakdown*.

How could Yolanda tell? She lay there. Mad, going mad, having a breakdown. This other narrative under every waking moment this other view staring back from every mirror. Brushing her hair for work, washing her teeth and seeing her familiar self, the same physical form but not that person. That being is no longer there. An older deeper face is staring back. Look, is this the face of someone who is this or is this the face of someone who comes from that. From that unspoken narrative who has walked out from a twisted dark history.

The moon was high in the sky through the windows of Yolanda's flat. It was a light in the sky but stone. Aircraft flew over the city each one carrying human bodies through the air. Stars were visible. She did not move. The moon did, the stars did. But did they? Or was it the earth spinning and sun rising and another day? Another day.

Another day of the window staring back at you. The sudden plunge always moments away and the madness descending every time a moment's hesitation gave a moment's peace. Then the rush of doubt and then the collapse of self, of this self. And if this self is gone, if this tower of Yolanda, daughter of Richard Jones, is gone what is there but a woman called Yolanda, muttering, 'Blow me away, blow me away,' on the streets of the city that takes in everyone, that holds its arms open to all the refugees from everywhere.

Natalie felt Tony come inside her and felt the flood of warmth. 'Umm, babe,' she said quietly and gratefully. He lifted up his head and she rolled him off her with her hands against his shoulders. He sat up and she sat up against the chair and collected up her knickers and pulled on her leggings. He looked at her and she reassured him, 'Sweet, babes, nice.'

Alan was aware that they had finished and unselfconsciously carried on fucking Sue. He drove into her harder and harder and emitted small groans. Her head bounced against the arm of the settee and he put his left hand on her neck. She said his name and slammed into her harder. He knew Natalie was watching and watching his hand on her neck and he slammed in harder again. Sue's next groan expressed some discomfort. Natalie pulled on her leggings with a bit more urgency. Alan ran his thumb across Sue's mouth and said, 'Come on,' and pushed her legs a little and he pushed into her and she put a hand down and clawed at Alan's belly and he came. He spilled into her and pulled out and Sue gave a sigh and felt all the tension dissolve and slipped away unconscious.

Natalie stood up and Tony said, 'What's up, Nat?' and she said easily, 'I'm getting back.'

'Hang on and have a drink,' said Tony, but accepting.

And she said, 'No – I'll get Wayne back down and I'll get off.' And she headed for the stairs.

Alan said, 'I'll have a drink,' and Tony poured themselves vodka and mixed in lemonade and Alan started rolling a spiff. Natalie bumbled down the stairs half carrying and half dragging the push chair with Wayne in it. The toddler was just awake. There was a small lightweight blanket folded on the back of the settee and Natalie put it over Sue. She bent down and said, 'Take it easy, babes.'

The young men watched her and Tony said, 'See you soon, Nats,' with a touch of friendly care.

And Alan said, 'Later, Nats.'

Natalie stored her knickers down the back of the buggy and pushed Wayne out into the night. In less than three minutes she was inside her own place and was unable to hear Tony and Alan's suppressed laughter as they mocked her in the kitchen of Sue's house.

Alan turned the music up and they drank and smoked and laughed and Alan mocked Tony and Tony mocked Natalie but not Alan or Sue. They laughed about Natalie's size and laughed about how quickly she left. They felt as if they were having a good time and woke up Ben. Ben had some vodka and smoked some spliff and they laughed about how he had missed it all.

Ben rummaged in his pockets and Alan and Tony watched as his face split into a smile and he pulled out a small flat square of thick magazine paper. He placed it on the kitchen work surface and began to open it announcing, 'Oooh look at that – a little bit of whizz.'

'Wicked,' said Alan.

And, 'Bet it's shit,' said Tony.

And Ben said, 'Nah it's alright – a bit scratchy but it's alright,' and they gathered around as the white powder was chopped into three lines on Sue's kitchen work surface and each of them bent over and inhaled the amphetamine up their noses.

Tony went last and stood up and started rubbing at his nose saying, 'A bit bloody scratchy, it's fucking shit, fucking shit,' and Alan and Ben gulped at their drinks as the taste of the sulphate trickled down their throats and Tony drank water straight from the tap and minutes later they were all talking loudly and moving their arms and legs in agitated movements and drinking more and more quickly.

John's body lay in the fridge. His flesh held all the scars of the years of no care. His liver was swollen and set in a surround of fat. His lungs were blackened and reduced. His big arteries hard and his guts distended and corroded. The ankle bone was half together and half apart. On his face were scars. John's hair was still slicked back, his teeth showing half rotten.

Outside Derek Gerrard was taunting Lucerne with all his internal pestilence and Lettie lay on the trolley waiting for her place in the fridge. Outside again anc the city hummed on, the hospital towering over its neighbourhood. From a hillside you could see the habitations all laid out and you saw a landscape punctuated by institutions, by hospitals and by prisons. Every road and every citizen knew these places, passed their doorways, and knew that in the hospital people die.

Derek Gerrard has his basement cauldron of fear to stir up, to frighten the two young nurses, to reach his sick inside and give himself a little thrill.

He slammed Lettie across to the elevating trolley and looked in Lucerne's face. She felt herself tense.

'I'm going to have to rearrange everything...' said Gerrard. Fondant looked away. Gerrard licked his lips. 'Someone will have to come out and move down so she can go in the top.'

The white tiles were clean although the grouting between them was discoloured in places. The refrigeration unit filled the space with its low spectrum hum. Gerrard's desk was in the corner. Past his desk and turning right was the post mortem lab with its slab and curved floor and drain. Gerrard's chair behind the desk was a high value executive swivel chair, upholstered in grey cloth and with prominent levers for adjusting height and tilt. There were two telephones on the desk and a large ledger open.

Gerrard walked around the corner into the post mortem lab. He came back pushing a second trolley. It was empty but it was also capable of elevating.

'Lucky this is still here,' he said, as he manoeuvred it into position by the fridges. He opened the fridge door and wound the trolley up to head height. He pulled out the tray and the corpse onto the trolley and pressed the button so the hydraulic pressure was released and the corpse sank slowly down to waist height on the trolley.

He then wound up Lettie's trolley to head height and pushed her into the vacated space. There was sweat on his upper lip and running out from his hairline by his ears.

'Well, she's sorted,' he said, 'I don't know what to do with this dirty fucker though.'

He tilted his head at John's body on the trolley. 'No one wants him.'

He puffed and sat down, 'I need you to sign the book.'

'What happens to him then?' said Fondant.

'Dunno,' said Gerrard. 'They'll probably cut him up. Find an excuse and chop him up for practice.'

'What about his family?' Fondant asked.

'Dirty junkie has probably robbed them all. No one wants him, darling. No one gives a toss. He is in here blocking up the system,' Gerrard paused, 'Do you want him?'

Fondant turned away. Lucerne signed the book on Gerrard's desk. He rubbed her entry with his finger and managed to stand close to her.

John's body lay on the trolley crowding the space.

Gerrard got past the trolley to the doors leading out of the morgue ahead of the two nurses. They were double doors but he held open just one side. They had to walk past him. Closely. He looked at the hair on Lucerne's neck where it swept up to her cap. He could smell her deodorant and see the little moles on her skin. Gerrard exhaled as she went past him. Fondant pushed past quickly in the wake of Lucerne and Gerrard turned quickly so he was square onto her back. His hand went down to adjust his genitals. Fondant almost tripped on Lucerne's heels as she rushed past him and just smelt his breath before the door closed behind her.

Gerrard went to his desk and sat down heavily. His thighs were almost bursting out of the surgical gown. John's body was on the trolley in front of the fridges. The shroud was still pinned shut over his face. Gerrard dialled an internal hospital extension. The line clicked through to an answerphone.

'This is Patient Affairs. If you have a message for Pat Driscombe, please speak after the tone.'

Gerrard was disappointed but as he had already gathered his thoughts and using his gently but firm official voice he carried on.

'Hi Pat. Further to the unsatisfactory situation regarding the unclaimed and unnamed corpse that is in the morgue. I must now further inform you that the situation down here is now such that I cannot any longer…'

He lost his way and allowed a pause before changing tone and pace and trying again.

'As you know Pat, you've been informed and not got back to me and with the situation here as it is I cannot see how I can continue to accommodate this in an ongoing situation.' He put the phone down but somehow it was not enough. He redialled and continued.

'Yeah, hi Pat – further to my earlier message I want to clarify this corpse is not currently in a cold unit but as an unregistered is held on the main floor. I look forward to hearing from you as soon as possible to take this situation forward. Many thanks, Derek.' He put down the phone satisfied.

He picked up his keys and stood up.

John lay on the trolley already beginning to warm up and rot. Gerrard walked out muttering something about showing that bitch up.

Yolanda picked up the phone. She dialled home. Her mother picked up, it was Gwen. 'Oh it's you,' she said.

'Yes, mother it's me,' said Yolanda.

'Oh, are you alright?' asked Gwen.

'I'm not sure,' said Yolanda.

'Oh – well - I'll get your father for you,' said Gwen.

It was crushing.

'What's wrong?' said her father's voice.

It didn't matter anymore. It didn't matter what was said, or done or anything anymore. She heard it in his voice and he heard it in her voice. She knew then and he knew then. There is no give in concrete.

Yolanda said, 'I'm not feeling right.'

And it could have been anything but Dr Jones told her, 'The thing is, Yolanda, you have always been unstable. We love you very much but you have always been prone to episodes... Your mother has worried herself sick over you, year after year.' He went on. Then he said, 'Have a word with your mother,' and Gwen told her to come home.

Yolanda put down the phone and walked over to the window. And opened the window. And looked down. And saw the paving stones where she would land. She saw where she would lie. Her hands and limbs shattered by the fall. She took two steps back. And walked up to the window and bent down from the waist and leant forward. Her head and torso were out over the ledge. Her weight was still down through her legs.

One push. Lean forward and one push. One shove. No scrambling back. Nothing to hold onto. No second thoughts. No regrets. Just a quick fall and done. Over. Peace. No more. No dirt. No shame. The sun was high in the sky.

Yolanda took two steps back. She left the window open. The room was now still. Completely and utterly still. Like a frozen moment that only one atom is moving in. As if all energy and all life is gone solid. Yolanda took two steps and picked up her phone. She called Michael. He was in. She asked, 'Michael – are you alone.'

He said, 'Yes, the kids are a school. Lyn's at work.' He was immediately nervous.

Yolanda continued, 'Michael, what would you do if someone hurt your girls.'

'Yolanda – what is this about?' Michael was worried now that this friend of his partner Lyn was asking him strange questions. But Yolanda sensed it and lightened up.

'No come on – what would you do?' she said in an almost childish tone and he was drawn in and said:

'Oh I don't know, chop off their heads, shoot them, you know something like that. Are you OK, Yolanda?'

'Yeah, I'm fine. I'm just writing a fairy story.' she said

and the conversation was over.

Yolanda walked to the window and looked out and down and left it open and ran a bath. She undressed and lay in the bath. She kept the bath hot by topping it up with hot water released by her toes working the tap. And every ten minutes she turned on the hot water with her toes.

Now there was no time or movement or pain and now she closed her eyes and in her hand she held a sword. A long curved Japanese sword and now it was heavy in her hand and the blade was sharp and glinting. Now Yolanda was strong and her arms were strong and now nothing moved as if there was blood in her veins, as if her heart was not beating. And she lay there and she called him and let him stand there before her. He saw her now free to act and he knew now that his time had come and that all the fear was his. Now it was not a child beaten with fear but a man of status and power and substance.

Yolanda stepped forward and he said *No* and she said *Dad* and the sword whipped through the air and his face fell away from his torso and Yolanda pulled out the gun and said *Mum* and it was if two shots rang out and she slumped and Yolanda stood over her and turned. There was Adrian and atoms colliding in a second and he was down and she gave him another one. And if her mother moaned another one. She walked up to the Elsworthy boy and shot him in the temple. And then the other one too.

The bedroom was still. The tap dripped. Yolanda shut he eyes again. She wanted to make sure no one was moving. His head lay six feet from his body. It was never going back. She was never going to move again. None of them. The sword was dripping with blood, the guns were smoking. It was done.

Ben was younger than Alan and Tony. He was not a rival to the older two or a threat to their friendship. He fitted in as admirer of both individually or as the junior of the three.

'If you had stayed awake Ben, you might have got a jump,' laughed Tony.

'How's that,' said Ben.

'I'm sure Natalie Parker would've gone again,' said Tony.

'As if,' replied Ben.

'Would have been a good way to pop your cherry,' said Alan.

'Oh get lost – I've done it loads,' Ben flustered up.

The older two knew Ben well enough to know that he had not. They knew he got scared around girls and knew his mates and knew his history and knew that of course he was a virgin. Tony and Alan were enjoying the game.

'Oh come on, Ben – Natalie's alright. Lovely tits mate. No questions asked with Natalie...'

'Nah – she doesn't do it for me,' said Ben.

'You saying I shagged a dog then?' Tony's tone was challenging but light.

'Nah – leave it out – you know what I mean, Tone.'

Ben was enjoying the game too, 'She's not exactly fit though – is she?'

'What about Sue?' Alan interrupted.

'Yeah, man Sue's fit,' said Ben, throwing the compliment at Alan really.

'Would you fuck her? Alan was mocking Ben.

'Oh she's hot.'

'Yeah, but would you do her?' Tony joined in.

Ben was laughing bit nervously but carried on, 'Yeah – course I would – I mean if she was up for it… I mean if she wasn't with you.'

Tony and Alan had been paying attention but somehow for a moment refilling glasses and getting another spliff together and adjusting the music took over.

Sue lay asleep on the couch with her face turned towards the back of the furniture. The light blanket that Natalie had put on her kept off the draught and a string of saliva dribbled out of her mouth.

Ben went upstairs to urinate and Emma came out of her bedroom crying. He said, 'Get back to bed,' and the child hesitated and Ben found enough iron in his voice to frighten her, 'Get in bed,' and as she turned around, 'And stop that bloody noise,' and muttered, 'Little bitch,' and went into the bathroom.

Downstairs Alan was telling Tony, 'Of course he's a fucking virgin,' and saying, 'Donna Andrews was my first.'

And Tony was saying, 'She was everyone's fucking first,' and they opened up the packet of magazine paper and found enough powder to make two lines. And Ben came back and they drank some more and sorted the last of the amphetamines and laughed about this girl and that girl and talked of sexual encounters, some real and some exaggerated half-truths.

The moon glared down at the city. The orb of dust was light and full in the sky. Night was lit up by the orange neon and electric pulses in glass bulbs. People slept and dreamt and a few danced and huddled in concrete stone corners you could always find a man in rags trying to sleep. Rats came out to attack black bags that smelt of food scraps.

Alan was chewing his lip. The amphetamine was accelerating the alcohol and the marijuana was opening up his circulation. Tony was ducking his head back and forth to the music. Ben was giggling a bit as Alan told him, 'I'm not with her. She's a fucking slag. She's a fucking slag.' The music pounded. Alan was trying to stretch his jaw muscles and trying to explain to Ben, 'She's a fucking whore – what's she done – she's a fucking slag – course she is.'

Ben was agreeing with Alan, Ben was keeping Alan's repetitive aggression at bay as the alcohol and the amphetamine raged through his system.

Tony kept repeating, 'Wicked, wicked,' at the music.

And Alan continued explaining to Ben, 'Just cos she is nice looking don't make her any different, just cos she is, you know, don't make her not a fucking slag for what's she done...' He paused and looked at Ben and challenged him, 'You know what I mean?'

'Yeah – hah – she's a fucking slag,' said Ben, licking his lips and feeling his teeth lock together.

'That's right,' said Alan, 'That right – that's why she is nothing to me, see.'

Tony released himself from the loop of the music and looked at Alan and at Ben and saw the intensity of their exchange and laughed and put his arm around Ben's shoulders and said, 'You going to fuck his bird then?'

And Alan picked up the beat, beat, beat of the music and swayed forward and back and laughed and said, 'Come on Ben – mate, you can fuck her.'

John lay on the trolley in the middle of the morgue and the morgue was at room temperature and he began to decay immediately. Minute by minute his skin discoloured and fluid seeped out of his rectum and inside the organs and intestines began to collapse and melt. His intestinal fluids began to eat away at the walls of his stomach and guts and gases bubbled and mixed in cavities and sludge gathered in veins and lungs and bladder and his physical being began to break down.

Derek Gerrard walked to the Spread Eagle public house. There were two men standing at the bar. Both had long lank hair.

One said, 'It's Deadly Derek,' and he and his companion laughed.

Derek ignored them and waited for his barman and then ordered his beer. He sat down at a corner table where he could see the television screen. A football match was being played. The two men at the bar were brothers. Derek had known them for ten years and they had known him. He opened up his evening newspaper on the table.

The football game dragged on. Derek ordered another beer and finished the paper and ordered another. A police car whizzed and whooped past on its way to a robbery. A middle-aged woman called Ann sat at the bar drinking vodkas, completing crosswords from a book of puzzles printed on the cheapest paper. Her skin was blotchy all over and her legs had ulcers showing on her shins. She wore shorts and sandals.

Derek went up to the bar for his fourth beer. The barman said, 'Same again?' and Derek nodded. The barman brought him a full glass of beer. Derek gave him a five-pound note and got coins in return.

'Busy day at work Derek?' asked one of the two long haired men.

'You could say so,' said Derek going back to his seat.

The one who had not spoken ordered two beers and a bag of peanuts. The football game was over, the barman was washing glasses.

The two men with long hair were brothers – or more accurately half-brothers. One with a round face was called John and the other with a thin face called Brian. Their mother had slept with her sister's husband – a man with a thin face while her husband's sported a gentle smile and round face.

The two men were locked together.

'Come and have a drink with us, Derek,' said Brian.

'No, I'm alright,' said the morgue porter.

'Don't be so bloody miserable, Derek – come on – I'll get one in for you.'

Derek puffed as if the offer of company and more beer was some kind of burden before standing up and acquiescing, 'OK, alright – I'll come up there,' and joining the two brothers at the bar.

Brian and John were long standing regulars in the Spread Eagle. Before long Derek had explained how there was a *situation* at work that he couldn't really talk about due to the serious nature.

Brian said, 'Well of course you can't say anything then.'

And John said, 'So what is it then?' and as another beer was ordered Derek reluctantly told them about the appalling mismanagement of Pat Driscombe resulting in a body left to deteriorate.

'Hang on a minute,' said Brian. 'But you're in charge, aren't you?' and Derek began to explain how he saw the chains of responsibility.

But John interrupted, 'Don't be stupid Derek,' and the beer was making him aggressive. 'You've come in here telling us how you are in charge of the morgue and suddenly you're passing it off onto someone else.'

'I am in charge,' said Derek.

'Exactly,' said John, and Brian continued

'So it's down to you. It's all down to you isn't it. You are in charge, aren't you?'

'Yeah, I'm in charge,' said Derek.

'So what are you going to do?' said John.

'Yeah, what are you going to do?' said Brian.

'Well,' said Derek.

'Well – you're powerless aren't you?' said John. 'You have been coming in here for years giving it the large – I am Mr Big at the hospital – and you can't actually sort out anything.'

'Sounds like you are one of those useless idiots only fit to sweep up the shit and change the bog rolls,' said Brian. 'Most organisations have them. And all the time some poor fucker is rotting away while you're in the pub drinking beer.'

John was sort of laughing and Brian was sort of laughing. There was a hyped atmosphere of drunken aggression. Derek was unfazed. He had not wilted at all.

Brian said, 'Shall I get another?' and the barman poured three beers and brought them over.

John supped his and said, 'It's a fucking disgrace.'

And Derek said, 'That's nothing, nothing at all.'

'No. Oh really – what else then?' said Brian.

'Well,' said Derek, 'it can go a lot further, a lot further.'

'What, further than letting a body rot?' said Brian.

Derek sipped his beer. He knew that they wanted to hear. He knew that the fascination of his tales fed into the lives of John and Brian, that he was a valued guest, despite the abuse, and that he had something they wanted. He waited until he had their attention, 'Well you know they do post mortems there?' he said.

'Yeah – so what?' said John.

'Well,' said Derek, 'Would you like to hold a human heart?'

Across the city more and more people were sleeping. Men and women slept alongside one another and babies lay comatose in cots. Children slept in bunk beds and the old retreated to their comfortable nests. Lights went out and all activity diminished across the streets and roads. But it never stopped and for some the working day began as others were living only in their dreams.

John and Brian were drunk and rowdy and loud and being amused by Deadly Derek Gerrard. Everyone else had left except for the barman and the woman drinking vodkas.

'Sorry Derek, what are you implying?' asked John.

'He's saying he can get hold of a human heart,' said Brian, as if interpreting.

'Is that what you mean?' said John.

Derek Gerrard took a slow mouthful of beer and looked at the two men with their long lank hair and glasses.

John was probably slightly older, nearer fifty than

Brian. He measured his words.

'In my position it would be entirely possible.'

John laughed out loud. Brian joined in. John addressed Derek directly and his face got closer to the other man's.

'Derek... are you saying you could open up a dead body and remove the heart?'

The two half-brothers went quiet and looked at Derek with mock full attention.

Derek repeated, 'As I said, it is entirely possible.'

John and Brian laughed. Brian took it another step further.

'So Derek – any chance we could have a look then?'

For a moment Derek lost his meaning before realising the other man was referring to a heart.

'Oh yeah – of course,' he said, entirely missing the mocking tone in Brian's question.

John joined in, 'Could you bring it here then?'

'Yeah of course,' said Derek.

'Oh great,' smirked John.

'Fantastic,' grinned Brian.

'No problem,' said Derek with a sort of authority.

'Wow!' said John.

'Tomorrow?' asked Brian.

'Should be OK,' said Derek.

'That is amazing, fucking amazing,' said John and Derek basked in the glow of their false wonder and didn't see John and Brian exchanging amused glances or have any sense of their derision.

Soon the barman was closing up the Spread Eagle and John and Brian were telling Derek, *Thanks for that*, and *Can't wait to see it*, and, *Until tomorrow*, and Derek headed back to his flat and lay down on his bed.

He was working out what time would be best to put John on the post mortem slab and what instruments to use to open up his thoracic cavity and how he would ift out the organ and cut away the arteries – he had seen it done, he had been there watching, he could do it – when he finally fell unconscious.

Dr Richard Jones was approaching retirement. He reflected that leaving the hospital and joining the health department was the finest strategic move of his life.

Now he was in the back of the chauffeured government car, with a national and international reputation as a health policy strategist. He mixed all day every day with powerful government men and reported directly to the elected minister. He worked closely with colleagues from other departments and lived in an expensed bubble where everything was arranged for him by the departmental staff.

He telephoned Geoff from the back of his car which was halted in traffic. He let Geoff know that Yolanda's mother was concerned about her. He called Bob Sanderson. Sanderson owned the publishing company that Yolanda worked for.

He telephoned someone called Lyn, a friend of Yolanda's, and telephoned Adrian to check that he was going to visit his sister. Then he telephoned Gwen and then he arrived at his appointment at the national police headquarters.

When he came out, he got back into the rear of the car. He pulled out a small dark blue box, the size of a matchbox, and opened it. Dr Jones took two tablets to manage his blood pressure. He phoned Gwen and confirmed that she had spoken to Yolanda and that the appointment was made. Everything was in place.

The car pulled up outside the department and Jones walked in. He never showed his identity card, daring the security men to challenge him. He took the lift to the fourth floor. His offices were next to the minister's. When he walked in, he said, 'Anything?' sharply to his personal assistant.

She said quickly, 'Bob Sanderson called and also a Dr Rudkin.' Jones went through to his large office and closed the door. He had no further appointments except for a thirty-minute feedback session with Annabel who was on the departmental graduate fast track development course and had been attached to his policy unit.

Jones walked across to the tall windows and looked out on the traffic pouring down to the broad avenue between blocks of government buildings. Buses, taxis, vans, private cars and bicycles were passing in two ceaseless streams. The sun bled down onto the stonework and pedestrians populated the pavements.

It was a city of millions, of millions of lives, millions of connections. A breeze flustered the plane trees and a few pigeons swooped on a dropped ham roll. The people of the city were from everywhere in the world. There were faces from the high mountains of South America and faces from the high mountains of Asia.

People, men women children, came from the deltas of the Far East, from the deltas of India, from the heart of Africa. Every country in Europe contributed, every part of America and every island every region and every continent. The whole world was in the city and those people lived side by side.

Randomly, by chance, like the dust particles blown in the wind people met. They found people from their own place or some place they had never heard of and man met woman and every day, and every moment of everyday a miracle took place as strangers became friends and with every sunrise light flooded the city and amongst the stone and the concrete and pulsing electric light men and women came together.

There is no pattern to the endless circulation of man and woman in the city, in the transport system, in clubs and bars, in homes and offices, in social groups or organisations but out of this comes the moment of quickening in the heart when love is felt and life is changed forever.

Yolanda walked past the open second floor window. Her mother was coming to visit tomorrow. With Adrian. Her mother was worried about her. Geoff had been asking if she was feeling alright and sneaking sidelong glances at her. He had stumbled around asking her if she has ever been unwell when she was growing up. Bob Sanderson had phoned her and suggested she take some time off if she ever needed it. Her father had called and reminded her that they all really loved her but were worried she was having another episode.

Lyn had come over to visit and as they sat drinking tea had talked about someone called Michelle who had mental health issues and was a really great person and something about how terrible the stigma was, but people who faced up to it were terribly brave. Lyn went and Yolanda lay down on the settee and closed her eyes, nothing had changed. The head lay six feet from the torso, the bodies with the gunshot wounds lay on the floor.

The Elsworthy boys were still dead.

Yolanda went and sat on the toilet. She barely needed to wee but for the one hundredth time that week she looked at the crotch of her knickers. There was nothing. No drop, no smear, no suggestion of the slightest pink, no sign of blood, no mark of womb lining being expelled. Nothing. She went and stood by the window and the sun roared its glory from the heavens and a bus went past with all the magnificence of ordinary lives. Yolanda breathed. Yolanda breathed.

Sue felt something prodding at her and felt sleep rising and falling from her. And then she let go back into unconsciousness and rolled on her back and felt a warmth between her legs and the room was rocking as she struggled to focus to see. There was something on her neck, pushing on her neck and a face close to hers and the ceiling was shifting up and down.

She let herself go and the prodding and the clamping on her neck and the shifting ceiling carried on but she was not there. She was not in that room alive but away just holding down the vomit and holding off consciousness and breathing and not hearing, not hearing. More than anything she did not want to hear.

It stopped and started again and she felt hands on her body, on her flesh pulling at her breasts and grabbing at her thighs. She let the drink take her away into a stupor of alcohol and dope and let every muscle stay loose and uttered not one word as it went on and her mind gripped only onto the vaguest image of the shadows of her daughters as they played on the swings in the playground in the park. Just their shadows.

And it went on and Sue knew it would end. She knew she could survive this. She knew that what was going down could be lived through as the pressure on her neck increased and the prodding and thrusting continued. Sue felt nothing but the weight of hands on her breasts, nothing but the push of a dead mass into her and no sense of time or the passing of minutes. It went on.

Things changed but it didn't stop. There was a slap and a different pressure and a different breath close to her face. She didn't want to hear and she didn't want to see as the settee rocked and the weight of one load of flesh became another weight of flesh and if she could stay away in the arms of the alcohol, of the marijuana, of sleep, of exhaustion, she would but she could not. She could not, not know.

She had to see a bit. Catch a glimpse for the record. Who was this that was talking vile filth at her, who was this that held her neck and who was pushing his dick into her. To see for a second was to sear your soul with a vision to haunt you, to revisit you, to come back and take you apart. Always it would be there.

There was no feeling, no sensitivity on her breasts, on her thighs, on her clitoris or vagina. Nothing felt like nothing. There was the rocking, the movement, the continued dull internal push. But nothing. To open her eyes, or even lift an eyelid, felt like the maximum effort. Why leave the warmth of the protective hood of stupor, of abuse, of not here at all, to take in even two seconds of the scene around the settee in her front room.

Not hearing was everything but sometimes it cut

through and she could hear panting and laughing and she fought to turn off the volume to not hear the crude talk, to not know they were saying she was loving it. Eyes closed and holding onto some certainty that it must end, like night does. Night does end, surely.

An assault again as the pitch of the noise gained a new urgency and a bolt of awareness shot through Sue as she heard a new direction to the snarling tone. She heard, 'Get up those stairs – go on – get out, you bitch,' and knows that her daughter has again retreated to her room. But Sue knows this will end and knows the small child has been scared away crying and has been hurt and Sue's heart is alive with that as the ceiling moves.

She didn't want to see who it was now. She didn't want to know or to remember any moments, any changes, any progress of time through it. It took everything to open her eyes for one second to see that the thing pushing at her now was Ben with his puppy fat chest and eyes and mouth screwed up as he panted and that the only thing to do was to live, to breathe.

It would end.

Derek Gerrard woke up early. It was four hours before he was due for work. He rolled onto his back and rested on his side and reached for the radio. He pressed the button and a talk station breakfast show started about the issues of the day.

Derek waited for the news at the top of the hour.

While he waited, he thought through his scheme. If he got in over two hours early no one would notice. There were no bookings in the PM lab and certainly no one would disturb him before nine. He knew where all the instruments were. Everything was there and he knew how to wash the place down afterwards.

He did not know the names of each instrument; he was not aware of their technically specified description but he had seen them used. The special large scissors and the stainless-steel saw. He knew where the special trays were kept for putting organs in. He had always had sets of clean green overalls and theatre shoes and gloves and hat. There was always a set of surgical scalpels to make the incision. He ran it all through his brain. The radio beeped a time signal and he sat up and swung his legs off the bed. He took off his T-shirt and underpants and walked naked to the bathroom. Derek looked at his corpulent mass with pride in the mirror. He washed his teeth and splashed a bit of water on his face. Then he put a fresh coat of deodorant on his unwashed underarms.

In the kitchen some clothes were drying on a rack. He picked up his socks, pants and a T-shirt. There was a pair of trousers draped over the back of the chair. He got dressed.

Fifteen minutes after waking Derek Gerrard was standing in the weak morning sun waiting for a bus. No one else was there and his face still wore a smirk. The bus pulled up and he boarded looking with contempt at the driver. He sat on the lower deck and regarded his travelling companions with distaste.

He breathed heavily and looked out the window at the shops and businesses and houses as the bus trundled through traffic lights and the beginning of the day's congestion. No one was going to do what he was going to do. No one was going to reach inside a body like he was. Gerrard smiled quietly in his corner thinking it through.

The bus stopped. Some early morning office cleaners got on. A uniformed delivery driver got off and headed to his depot. A cluster of men stood outside the train station in high visibility jackets. An ambulance was driven over to the side of the road and the driver and attendant were dozing waiting for their next call.

As Derek Gerrard thought through his scheme it was his removal from the banal and ordinary that drove him. He looked around at the passengers on the bus, he looked out of the window at the ordinary and everyday and he knew he was special, extraordinary, a level above. He could do what he wanted and he could do this. It was only two more stops and then he would disembark and approach the building and begin his task.

The hospital had the main entrance and reception. It also had the entrance to the emergency and accident facility. And downstairs there was the main delivery area where all the lorries and vans would deposit all the goods for the cargoes and supplies to keep the institution alive. All these entrances were busy and staffed and regulated. Down here were also the kitchens and the chefs left open the back door. Derek Gerrard walked in and headed for the morgue.

He walked down the corridor seeing nothing or anyone. People passed him and he passed the laundry and the lab and the stores and the maintenance crew. Derek Gerrard was floating on his self-importance on his specialness on his self-appointed gravitas and inside he hummed with aliveness. Finally he could see the double doors and reached for the keys.

Derek Gerrard paused and reflected on his position and what he was going to do. He was going to show a lot of people something that he had always known. It was something that gave him an inner strength and blasted out his certain glamour.

The morgue porter, Derek Gerrard, had power a special power, and now he was going to show the world. Now he was going to cut out a human heart. His hand went inside his pocket.

Gwen stood in Yolanda's flat looking at her daughter. Adrian stood behind her left shoulder. Gwen hated the city and hated being made to spend a day on public transport and away from her house and glass of wine to relax. Her face was fixed and sour. Dealing with this troublesome girl was an unwanted pressure. It had to be done, Richard was right.

Some part of Yolanda had hoped that her mother's visit might be the precursor to change, that this first visit alone to her place might be the start of a new footing between them. For Gwen to make time for her, for her mother to come to her without her father, for all these firsts Yolanda had constructed a world of possibilities. Perhaps from the wreckage she could salvage something.

'If you're ready then,' said Gwen, 'We'll get going. I have to get the four-thirty train back.'

Yolanda packed up her handbag. She opened it and fished out her keys. Adrian didn't say anything and the three of them walked the four hundred metres to the medical practice in silence. The sun shone and the streets were quiet.

The doctors was a general practice, a group of doctors amalgamating their resources and patients in a modern single-storey block on the corner of a street of terraced three-storey houses. The block housed nurses and dentists as well as consulting rooms and the reception area and a large room of files and records. Every morning the reception would fill up with sick people who would be seen by the doctors at a rate of four or five per hour. At one pm it was all over and the doctors would take lunch.

After lunch the building stayed closed and the doctors went to meetings and home visits and to the hospitals.

Patients were allowed in to see the dentists or the nurses but the reception was quiet now. It was two o'clock and Yolanda sat with her mother while Adrian stood at the counter.

Yolanda watched the fish in the fish tank that was on a shelf behind a row of chairs in the seating area. Her mother sighed with impatience. Adrian came back and sat down and picked up a magazine. Yolanda glanced at Gwen and looked away. She saw her mother's dried skin and mouth set grimly and dissolute unhealthy eyes. She wondered why she was here. Why had her mother said 'We're going to pop into the practice?'

Dr Rudkin came into reception through a grey door. She was slim and smart and giving off the air of competence and busy busy. Gwen stood up and Adrian stood up and by the time Yolanda had got to her feet Rudkin was speaking with Gwen. 'If you go down now, they are expecting you. There may be a wait but I have spoken with them. Here's the letter,' and she held out a brown envelope. Adrian took it. Rudkin looked at Gwen and then at Adrian. Neither of them spoke.

Yolanda said, 'Wait a moment – what's this.'

Rudkin said, 'People are concerned – just go along.'

A shadow of pity crossed the doctor's face and she said to Gwen. 'The wait can be difficult but...' and she turned away and walked out of reception and through the grey door.

Adrian looked down at the letter in his hand and he looked pleased with himself. He had accomplished something here; his father would be proud of him. He had the letter.

Outside Gwen and Adrian started walking and Yolanda followed. Yolanda was saying, 'Hold on, where are you going?'

And Gwen said quietly to Adrian, 'Get a taxi,' and turned to her daughter and said, 'You need to buck up – don't get hysterical, you'll make it worse.'

'I'm not hysterical,' said Yolanda.

'Not yet you're not,' said Gwen.

A single magpie croaked its strange squawk squeak from a rooftop and two young mothers stood smoking on the street corner, their baby buggies alongside each other.

'You can't do this,' said Yolanda.

'Calm down,' said Gwen 'It's just a check-up. Calm down or you'll make it worse.'

'Make what worse? What's going on?' There was panic in her voice.

'You have to have a check-up. We're taking you to the hospital now. Try to stay calm or you'll make it worse.'

Adrian had hailed a cab. It pulled over and its diesel engine was ticking over with an occasional irregular shudder. Adrian got in, Yolanda hesitated. Gwen gripped her arm. She held it hard so it hurt and said, 'Get in, now.'

Yolanda got in and her mother got in after her. Yolanda's mind began to race.

She spoke, 'This is all bullshit. Rudkin never even looked at me. There's nothing wrong with me.'

'You're getting agitated,' said Gwen.

'I'm not going – I'm not going anywhere,' said Yolanda.

'If you don't go, they have to call the police,' Adrian spoke flatly, dully without emotion.

'What?' said Yolanda.

'If you don't show up, they have to cover themselves. They'll tell the police.' Adrian was matter of fact about it.

'Don't be fucking stupid,' said Yolanda.

'Ssh, ssh. Be quiet,' said Gwen 'That's half the trouble, Yolanda – getting agitated.'

Her daughter looked out the window of the taxi at the people walking, at the people at the bus stop, at people going about their everyday living and Yolanda breathed as the sun shone from a sky peppered with white clouds.

'I don't understand. Why would they call the police?' Yolanda was controlling herself and directed the question at Adrian.

'Because everyone's worried that you might do something stupid.'

'Like what?'

'I think they say be a threat to your own or other people's safety.'

The taxi was at traffic lights. The phrase reverberated around Yolanda's skull. It was legal speak. It was official language that Adrian was regurgitating. The process was underway. Yolanda felt a terrible heaviness creeping over her. The heaviness was washing over her. The taxi was moving again.

'What's the letter say?' asked Yolanda.

Gwen answered, 'It's that Rudkin asking for a check-up

at the hospital.'

Yolanda knew that her mother was telling her a lie or at the very best a deceitful half-truth.

She sat back and tried to somehow assess her situation but the taxi pulled up outside the hospital accident and emergency department and she stood there with her mother as Adrian paid the driver with cash and waited for a receipt.

'Come on,' said Gwen, and they walked to the hospital reception area and Yolanda watched as Adrian gave her name and address. The receptionist glanced at Yolanda and looked away embarrassed. She took the letter from Adrian and they all went and sat on chairs in the waiting area.

There were possibly a total of twenty people waiting.

Yolanda sat apart from her mother and Adrian. The letter from Rudkin was clearly going to sink her. And her mother and her brother. Two relatives and a recommendation from your doctor and a threat to yourself or others.

Yolanda was going to lose her liberty, was going to lose her life in the city. It was being taken away. She looked around and looked at the doors. She could run – but then she knew how it would be escalated, how he could play that even better. The heaviness sat on her. How long would it be before they took her away.

How long would it be before she was taken away to a ward, to a room full of mad people and given pills and maybe injections? How long had she got? Maybe an hour.

Sue lay staring at the ceiling. It was quiet. The music had stopped. The room smelt of smoke and alcohol and sweat and sex. Cigarettes and spliffs had been dropped on the floor and trodden in. Ashtrays had been spilt. A glass had been broken and alcohol spilt.

The sun was shining. Birds were singing.

Traffic was going down the road. People were beginning to move.

Sue pulled the small lightweight blanket up but her lower legs were getting cold. Her clothes were not within reach. She could see her bra across the room on the floor.

There was nothing she wanted. She didn't want Will; she didn't want to remember anything. She didn't want to get up and she didn't want to get dressed. Sue wanted the quiet and the unmoving and not to be touched. Not to be disturbed or have to do anything ever. Ever again.

She turned onto her side and tried to drag some warmth from the blanket. Her skin was goose bumped and she tried to close her eyes but wanted them open and fixed on the wall. The wall was not moving. The wall was not alive and Sue wanted that inert certainty.

The sun rose higher in the sky and more traffic moved and more people in the city woke up and some finally began to close down and sleep. Some would sleep through the day and wake again at night and Sue stared coldly at the wall.

There was a movement upstairs. There was the sound of a door opening and small footsteps moving around. Another door opened upstairs and the sound of the bathroom being used. Then the fast light thumps of small young feet across the floor. And then a young voice exclaiming, 'Oh,' and more moving and you could just discern children's voices.

Sue did not move. She lay there staring at the wall unwashed, naked beneath the blanket. There were crows in the trees at the edge of the estate. Big black birds slowly circling and watching for carrion, for dead flesh. They cried out to one another as the sun rose and people left their houses to work, to gain money for life.

Emma woke up Sharon and said, 'It's OK they've gone.'

And Sharon said, 'Where's Mummy?' and Emma didn't really know but wanted to get dressed anyway because she really wanted to go to school and not be in the house.

Emma knew they had clean socks and pants in their drawer because Mummy always put them there on Sunday night. They put on the uniform pinafore dresses over the same shirts they had worn the day before. Sharon said, 'Can I have a clean one?'

And Emma said, 'No wear that one, it doesn't matter,' because she knew her mother had not washed and dried their shirts earlier in the week.

They stood in front of the mirror in Sue's room and brushed their hair. Emma put elastic ties and clips into her sister's hair before brushing her own back into a ponytail. Emma was satisfied that now they would be able to go to school. And they went downstairs together.

At the bottom of the stairs the door to the living room was ajar. Emma pushed it open. Sharon saw her mother on the settee and exclaimed, 'Mum,' and ran to her and jumped onto the settee and tried to lie down beside her.

Emma stood by the door looking at the mess and her mother naked under a small light blanket and the cigarette butts on the floor and her mother's clothes here and there and glasses of alcohol with ash floating in them. And her mother's face and hair tired and a mess. 'I want to go to school,' she said.

Sue pushed Sharon away but her daughter clung on and Sue had to grapple her away.

'I want to go to school,' repeated Emma determinedly and as a rebuke to her mother.

Sue managed to sit up. Sharon tried to get close and was pushed away again. Sue wanted to lie down and look at the wall in quiet. She wanted no noise, no movement, no memory, no nothing.

Gerrard's podgy fingers pulled out the key. He unlocked the mortice lock and tapped in the numbers on the security lock. He pushed open the first set of doors and then pushed open the righthand side of the double doors. The fridges hummed on, the tiles gleamed under the nonstop twenty-four/seven electric lights. Between his desk facing him on the left and the back of fridges to the right was the trolley.

A body lay on the trolley. A man's body in a shroud of white hospital cotton, the face panel cover pinned shut. The rooms were filled with the hum of fridges and a nasal layer of chemical disinfectant just tainted with a tiny percentage of the sweet filth of a deteriorating corpse.

Derek pulled the trolley past his desk and swung it round the right. Here was the slab. Here was the place to carve up the human body. He went back to his desk and opened his top drawer and took out a small bunch of keys. With these he opened the drawers beneath a long counter opposite the slab and opened the walk-in cupboard with its shelves of folded clean surgical greens. The shirts on one shelf and the trousers below.

He took off his unwashed jeans and unwashed sweat

shirt and took off his damp shoes. As he bent over, he puffed and groaned a little. He pulled on the clean green trousers and tied them with the clean white cord. Gerrard put on the green shirt and tied it at the side with bows. He put his feet in the slip-on plastic theatre shoes. He pulled down a green hat from the top shelf and picked up a face mask. These items he placed on the counter top.

Derek Gerrard went back to his desk and picked up the key for the mortice lock. He went over to the doors and opened the first set and locked the outer set with the key. He left the key in the lock. No one could get in. He checked the time. No one would even phone for another three hours. Now was the time to get started.

He walked back past his desk and round to the right. The tubes of neon pulsed light down through ceiling tiles diffusing it across every part of the room. There were to be no shadows or crevices on any service. The concrete floor was gently concave and then there was the drain. The walls were tiled white. He put on the brakes and walked around the other side of the slab. He reached over and grasped the shroud and pulled the body onto the marble bed.

Gerrard went to the long counter and opened the top drawer. Then he opened the second drawer. All the tools were in sealed plastic packets, all newly disinfected and cleaned and spotless. He put on the hat. He walked around the body. He walked back to his desk. He went and checked that the mortice lock was locked and the key was in the lock.

Behind his closed doors, and in his special clothes, Derek Gerrard was emperor and king. Outside the city went on, outside the hospital went on in this room now, in this place, in this one multiple square footage Derek Gerrard was in total control. The man, who could do what he wanted. He could do anything. And he would.

Yolanda sat apart from her mother and her brother. She was watching the receptionist and the nurses who would call patients by name to be examined. They would be escorted down a corridor to a booth. That was all she could see. Then doctors would visit the booth. Most of the people waiting had visible injuries. A couple looked very sick. There were two children with parents and a babe in arms.

As far as Yolanda could estimate her process would be to go to a booth and be seen by a doctor and then taken to a ward. The ward would be full of deranged people and the nurses would give her drugs. If she ran away the police would be called. Everybody would say there were worried about her and everybody would say they loved her. Then they would leave her in a room full of hyped-up mentals and advise her to take pills.

She closed her eyes. She wanted to rerun the scene with the sword and hear the boom of guns despatching them. Yeah, it was still there. Boom, boom, take that, so she felt it and looked at Gwen and Adrian and said:

'Is it OK if I pop to the loo?'

And watch them glance at one another for assurance and Gwen said, 'Of course it is,' and Yolanda sat on the toilet and looked at the crotch of her knickers and there was nothing there and she breathed. She breathed and she found some part of iron in her soul saying you can hurt me but not my child, not my child. She went back out to the waiting room, and stared at the ceiling and closed her eyes and it was as if she could smell the smoke of the gunfire and they were not moving now – they were done.

She saw a nurse talking to the receptionist. The receptionist handed her the letter from Rudkin. The nurse walked away with the letter. Yolanda looked at her brother and looked at her mother. They were going to poison her child with psycho pharmaceuticals. She closed her eyes.

The nurse was walking towards them. She looked at Yolanda, assessing her from head to toe. As she arrived, she put on a professionally pleasant smile and said, 'Hi – are you Yolanda's family?' addressing Gwen and Adrian.

Gwen said, 'Yes.'

And the nurse said, 'This shouldn't take too long, the doctor is coming down,' and then she turned to Yolanda and said, 'Yolanda, come along with me,' and turned and hesitated for half a moment to make sure her patient was acquiescing and Yolanda followed her past the reception desk down the corridor and the nurse stood and gestured Yolanda into a booth that had a chair and a trolley bed in it. Yolanda went into the small space and the nurse stood by the entrance, there was only a curtain that was not drawn, and said, 'Dr Rose is coming down. She really won't be long. Just make yourself comfortable,' and the nurse walked away.

For a moment Yolanda perched on the side of the trolley bed and then sat on the chair. Then she got up and went to the entrance to her booth and looked out into the corridor. To the left the corridor went back out to reception and to the right was the nurses' station where she could see her nurse on the phone and piles of brown files stacked around the desk.

She sensed a presence to her left. She took half a pace

forward and could see a young man in the booth next to hers. He was rocking back and forward and muttering and clicking the light switch on the wall on and off, on and off, repeatedly. He looked clean and was shaved and was muttering and clicking the light switch on and off. His other arm was tense and moving his other hand up and down from waist to shoulder.

Yolanda stepped back. She breathed. She went and sat on the chair. It was that difficult time when mad people were taken off the streets and locked up by the mental health professionals operating the mental health system. Under some section of the law people could be detained and so they called it *sectioning* and by the law you could be detained with the consent of two relatives and a doctor.

In the interests of efficiency, the hospital liked to do all the sectioning that was required each day at three-thirty pm. The police, the doctors, the ambulances, the families could then get their mental cases to the hospital to be locked up, sedated, drugged all at the same time by one doctor in one swift turn of duty.

Now Yolanda's time had come.

Sue traipsed up the hill behind her two daughters. Emma looked over her shoulder and said, 'Come on mum.' Sharon wanted to hold Sue's hand but Emma said, 'Come on, if we walk quickly, we won't be late.' Ahead they could see a mother pushing a buggy and hurrying a seven-year-old boy along. All the rest of the children were in school already.

When they reached the last one hundred metres from the school gate Emma took Sharon's hand and said, 'Come on, let's run,' and she turned and looked at her bedraggled mum, said, 'Bye mum,' and ran in to school.

Miss Ferdinand had just sat all the children down when Sharon came in the door and hesitated, standing still. Miss Ferdinand greeted her warmly and immediately could see that the child was looking tired and unkempt. Sharon was never late and was always smartly turned out with her hair clean and neatly tied. She was showing the signs of their being problems at home.

Emma went into her class and quietly sat down next to her best friend Sarah Hattab. Sarah smiled at her and said, 'Get your reading book out.' Outside you see across the playground and through the chain link fencing the pavement. You could see Sue turning back down the hill and heading towards the estate. She was walking slowly through the still city air. A smartly dressed man walked up the hill on the other side of the street and a courier van appeared around a corner, changed gear and pulled noisily away.

Sue went into the small shop on the corner of the block and looked at the Asian shopkeeper. He was a middle-aged man and a veteran in the business. He looked at her closely. Sue felt his stare and dug into her jeans pocket for money. She ordered a small pack of cigarettes and a can of Coca Cola. He handed her the loose coins in return for her note and said nothing. It was as if he could see the alcohol and dirt on her. She said, 'You seen enough?' with a slur and a faltering anger as she turned and left the small space.

In the last ten minutes before playtime, Miss Ferdinand liked to gather her class around her chair, the children sitting on the floor cross-legged. She asked, 'Has anyone got any news, has anyone got something to tell us.' It was an opportunity to get the children to speak, to explain and to share. Then they would sing a song and go out for twenty minutes of free play and running around in the playground.

Sharon was sitting in the front. She generally did and she was often a keen contributor to this part of the day. Miss Ferdinand has noticed her quietness all morning and was not surprised that she had nothing to say. Now as she looked at her, her eye was caught by something on the child's leg. On the inside of her leg, from just about her knee to just below it, there was a line about four inches long of a dried viscous fluid.

When the children were sent out Miss Ferdinand called Sharon over. She took out a make-up wipe from her handbag and said, 'Come here, left me get this,' and squatted down in front of the small child and wiped away the dried-up fluid stain. 'What was that?' she asked Sharon gently and the child just sort of shrugged and Miss Ferdinand found herself looking further up the child's leg. There was nothing else to see. Sharon went and joined the other children.

Miss Ferdinand went into the staffroom for a cup of coffee during lunch and playtime. She was shaken up. She knew, she had a boyfriend, she knew. There was a familiarity with the way that stuff was on her skin that was pouring fear into the young teacher's system. She sat down and gathered her thoughts. Why had she wiped it away? What was it? How could you be sure?

Sue Smith sat down next to her and said, 'You've got Emma Smith's sister, haven't you?'

Miss Ferdinand sighed and turned to look at Sue, 'Yes,' she said.

'Things are not looking right, are they?' said the older

girl's teacher.

And Sharon's Miss Ferdinand said wearily, 'I'm really worried.'

There was a silence. Both women knew this was dangerous ground, that being concerned, worried or noting warning signs put an obligation on them to report, and that reporting would trigger procedures and intervention and the certain destruction of Sue's little family.

'It's only been a few days,' said Sue Smith.

'I know,' said Miss Ferdinand.

'Have you spoken to her?' asked Smith.

'No.'

'Will you?'

'If I can catch her,' said Miss Ferdinand, and she looked away from Smith and thought about the stuff on the child's leg and thought about how the child seemed unfocused and how the child's concentration was gone and how she had sat there all morning completely and utterly absent.

Out in the city the narcotic traders were waking up for another day's profit taking. Sue walked back onto the estate as Patrick and Megan shuffled out of their door to start looking for a fix. In the chemists a pharmacist handed out a cupful of synthetic heroin to a one-legged man in a wheelchair and in the doctors, a scared looking woman sweated asking for her repeat prescription. On the seventeenth floor of a tower block of flats a prostitute who called herself Crimson was crying with frustration, unable to get in a vein on her foot.

A woman patrolled outside the parade of shops with twenty carrier bags; each filled with used plastic bags. She moved her bags two by two up the road and then returned for another two. She smelled and the bags smelled and her skirt boasted stains of excrement. A man stepped past with a lampshade on his head and shoppers moved aside. Sue walked on past and the sun still blazed down.

Derek Gerrard set to work. He cut the shroud from head to toe and peeled the white cloth back. He walked around the body, folding back the white material. Methodically he pulled it away from under the body until the corpse lay naked on the slab. He scooped up the cloth into a green bag marked recycled waste and put it in the corner.

He breathed down heavily into his mask, beads of sweat running down from his hairline. He went to the counter and picked up a plastic packet with three scalpels of varying sizes. He had plastic shields over their blades. Gerrard selected the biggest one and removed the shield and lay the instrument down on the counter top.

The body had begun to discolour where you see soft flesh and tissue. Then black shadows and a touch of purple around the shoulders and on the thighs. There was without a doubt the taste of deterioration in the air. Droplets of evaporating odour were flavouring the room.

The flesh on the face was falling back onto the bone. The cheeks were falling into the cavities below the skull shape around the brain. Somehow the neck was too flat on the marble, at the wrong angle from the chest – Derek Gerrard put his hand on the chest looking for the sternum.

Now he suddenly felt unsure. Should he open up the ribcage by hacking up from the sternum to the throat, cutting through all that bone or should he split open the flesh below the ribs and go in there. Lying in bed he had thought it through simply enough but now the mechanics and connections and angles seemed less clear. He took two paces back and looked again.

He went to the drawer and took out the short stainless-steel saw in its plastic pack and the big scissor-like tool. Again, he reviewed the body. He went up to it and prodded under the ribs on the left side and felt the central join of the ribcage. Somehow he wasn't quite sure how to get started.

Gerrard pushed down on the ribcage and somehow the head moved. He started and stepped back. There seemed to be a sudden closeness and lack of air in the room. He wiped the sweat off his forehead with his forearm and went over to the counter and picked up the biggest scalpel. He returned to the body and tried to position himself to make the first cut. Somehow he could not arrange his arms in such a way as to be able to apply pressure. He stood back and straightened up.

He looked at the body from head to toe and leant forward again resting his right elbow near the neck and dropping down his hand and scalpel to cover the sternum. He focused and concentrated and watched the blade go into the flesh and cut a half inch incision. No blood came out.

The morgue porter stepped back again. He was going to have to expand that cut and then start breaking open the thorax. Derek Gerrard glanced up at the clock on the wall. There was plenty of time. He stepped forward. His groin was in line with the shoulders. He began to line up the scalpel.

The refrigeration unit hummed and hard surfaces on the floors and walls locked in every sound, every footstep, every breath. Outside the morgue the night shift of nurses were handing over to the early day shift and the kitchen was in full flow and the laundry men were loading machines. The lift mechanism whined and the pharmacy was being opened up. If there was an overnight death the body would be kept on the ward until the morgue opened. It was not open yet.

Derek Gerrard was going to lengthen and deepen his original cut. He wanted to apply more pressure down through his arm so he shifted his feet a little. His sightline was down over the ribcage, past the pubic area and the body's penis to the thighs and feet.

Gerrard leaned forward and put his elbow by the throat and began to drop down his hand. It was just a practice run to estimate the required movement. It worked fine. His hand came back up. He breathed as sweat dropped off his face. His eyes ran down the body but strayed off the torso and looked at the left arm.

Below the elbow in the inside of the arm was something. A mark that was not quite discernible. Gerrard looked closer. It was faded blue marks. It was a home-made tattoo on the soft flesh of the inside of the forearm. There were four badly formed letters and some numbers.

Dr Clare Rose was the duty psychiatrist. The purpose of sectioning was to get patients up onto the psychiatric wards for full assessment. Once admitted a full understanding of the patient's condition could be gained. As the consultant had said to her, 'It might be a distressing moment for the families, but in reality, it's far less serious than being admitted for an ingrowing toe nail.' Some days there was no one to see at three-thirty and some days there were four or five to see. Today there were just two.

She came to Yolanda's booth first and introduced herself. The letter from the family doctor explained that the patient was suffering from a psychotic episode and needed admission as family members were concerned, she was a possible threat of harm to either herself or others. The psychiatry team had a policy of positive intervention and Dr Clare was not about to start taking risks. She began asking Yolanda the standard questions to assess her state of confusion and agitation.

'Hi Yolanda – how are you feeling?' and, 'I know it's a stressful time – do you know what day of the week it is today?'

'Ah fine, thanks Yolanda. I wonder can you tell me who the prime minister is?'

'Great – now are you feeling very anxious? Do you think someone else is manipulating events?'

Yolanda looked up into the face of the doctor. She was a woman of almost forty who lived in a suburb and probably lived in a house like her father's. Dr Clare had the training and the monthly pay cheque and the big house that told her she knew what was best.

'No, I don't feel that at all,' lied Yolanda.

'Do you have feelings of threat or of harm to other people?' asked the doctor.

Yolanda thought of the sword, of the head lying feel away from the body, of the booming gunfire, the inert bodies, the smell of gun smoke.

'No, not at all,' she said.

'Umm,' said Dr Clare as if *Umm* meant something. 'Well people are very concerned about you, Yolanda – it might be best if you come in for a couple of days while we can see if we can get to the bottom of this.'

Yolanda looked at her. Dr Clare felt something in her gaze and continued. 'Have you ever had suicidal thoughts?'

Yolanda let the question hang in the air. She thought of the possibility of something growing inside her, of her unbloodied knickers and she thought of the window and the plunge to the pavement and she looked up into the doctor's face and saw nothing but a threat to her child. Someone who was going to not only harm her but harm her tiny heart growing somewhere deep inside her.

'No, I'm a generally optimistic person,' she answered levelly.

'Good, good,' said Dr Clare. 'That's good. I'm going to book you in then – I'm sure we've got a bed and I'll speak with your mum too.' The doctor reached forward and stroked Yolanda's arm with her hand. Yolanda looked at the doctor's hand on her arm and breathed and held back everything, and breathed.

Outside there were blue afternoon skies over the city and aircraft and helicopters below them and floating up from the city some balloons with paper tags with children's wishes on them. Yolanda could hear Dr Clare saying, 'Don't worry – this is what everyone thinks is best for you,' in her professionally empathetic and caring voice as she turned away to take the next steps.

The sun broke through a cloud and the balloons rose higher from the hands of children standing outside a single-storey hut beside a railway line. The children watched the balloons rise and one girl said, 'I can't see any angels.'

Another child said, 'You can't ever see angels, they're magic,' and the woman looking after them laughed at the moment, the minute of joy, the second of happiness grasped from that day.

Yolanda looked left out of the booth, left past reception, at Dr Clare speaking with Gwen and Adrian. She went back and sat on her chair and moments later heard Dr Clare begin talking with the person next door who was still flicking the light switch on and off. She wondered vaguely if her mother and Adrian were still there or had left already. She was looking at the floor between her legs. She heard Dr Clare finish with the person next door.

'Hi,' said a voice, and Yolanda looked up. A woman with short but full curly blonde hair stood in the doorway. She wore a short checked skirt over black tights and flat shoes. Around her neck dangled official hospital identification. Her skin was smooth, her eyes clear grey and she wore red lipstick.

'Oh, hi!' said Yolanda.

'You OK?' asked the woman in an accent that was American.

'Yeah – I am OK,' said Yolanda. The American woman laughed, lightly, musically.

'OK,' she said, 'So why are you here?'

Somehow Yolanda managed a short heavy laugh. 'Well,' she said and left volunteering anymore or going any further.

It was quiet. You could hear the light switch being flicked on and off and you could hear the sound of the hospital, but in the space between Yolanda and the woman standing in the doorway of the cubicle of the hospital there was not a sound, only silence.

'Well,' said the voice with an American accent. 'Sometimes there is just a single moment in time. Just one moment when something is possible. Trust me. Do you trust me?'

Yolanda sat up and back on her chair and looked at the good-looking blonde American standing in the doorway.

Sue walked back onto the estate. A white wall was dedicated to a youth killed by a single knife strike inflicted over a drug debt and in a corner where two low walls met was a collection of empty cans of strong lager and discarded cigarette packets. Sue sat on the single swing on the patch of grass a hundred yards from her front door. Sue smoked a cigarette and looked at her feet pushing her backwards.

Natalie looked out of her kitchen window and saw Sue on the swing and opened her front door and shouted, 'Hey Sue,' but her friend either ignored her or pretended not to hear. Natalie went back and got her flip-flops on and came out with Wayne on her hip.

'Sue,' she said firmly, as she approached and Sue let her feet drag on the floor so that swing slowed down and she turned and looked.

'Sue – you alright?' asked Natalie.

Sue got off the swing and stood up. She walked over to Natalie until she was just a yard away and said, 'Of course I'm alright,' and walked away.

Natalie said after her, 'Hang on, Sue. Sue, come back,' and took three steps after her before pausing and stopping. She watched Sue walk between the two blocks of maisonettes until she reached her door. Sue fished the key out of the back pocket of her jeans and opened the door to her place. She went inside and lay down on the settee.

Wayne started moaning and crying and Natalie went back inside her front door. She wanted to wash some clothes but she had no washing powder. She sat Wayne down on the floor and sat on her settee. There was something wrong with Sue. She knew that. She knew that Sue was in trouble. Natalie wanted to go and knock on Sue's door but she was scared that Sue would say, *What do you want?* in her accusing tone because Sue knew that Natalie had no money and that until Natalie got her cheque even a cup of tea, even a biscuit and a piece of toast was supporting Natalie and who was she to tell her anything.

Natalie chewed her fingernails and went into the kitchen. In the fridge she had an open can of soup. She warmed the soup and pulled Wayne onto her lap. Down the side of the settee, between the arm and the cushions she pulled out a rolled-up bag of crisps. She dipped the pieces of crisp into the soup and fed them to Wayne.

Ben slept on a mattress on the floor in the room he shared with his brother Miles. Miles had the single bed against the opposite wall. The bed had not been slept in for months. Their mother Di shouted at Ben, 'Get up,' and the boy dressed himself and went downstairs.

'There's two quarters of black there on the side with the VO,' his mother instructed him. 'Don dropped them round. He said you'll be fine with it in your mouth. No problem at all.'

Ben picked up the prison visiting order and the two pieces of hash. His mother said, 'Here's my travel card,' giving him her pass for public transport. 'And tell that daft brother of yours I love him very much.'

Ben walked out of his house and around the corner and walked past Sue's and walked past Natalie's and out onto the road and stood waiting for a bus to take him to the train station. He would get off the train and get another bus and then enter the prison and the prison visitors' waiting room. Then he would go into the custody room and there would be the thrill of passing the stuff over and then giving the messages for Don and then he would get the bus and the train and the bus back.

His mum would ask him about Miles and Don would come round and see him. Then he would sit indoors and hope that he could watch the television without Alan or Tony coming round.

All day Miss Ferdinand watched Sharon and not once did the child play with her friend or show any sign of animation. When the school day had just thirty minutes left to go Miss Ferdinand called out, 'Tidy up time,' and the children would run around, racing to put drawing, painting and craft materials away in their designated boxes.

Rather than being one of the keenest organisers saying crossly, 'Not there, not there,' Sharon stood by idly at her table looking out of the window.

Miss Ferdinand was about to chide her about it but instead caught her attention with a firm but gentle, 'Sharon,' and indicated for the child to come over to her with a crooked finger. Sharon walked over slowly and Miss Ferdinand picked her up and sat her on her lap. The girl relaxed with the warmth of her teacher's body. The stress left the child's body and she shifted on Miss Ferdinand's lap and felt completely safe.

The rest of the children shuffled around and their teacher offered comments of praise and thanks as tables were cleared and order restored. Miss Ferdinand looked down at the child on her lap and from nowhere said, 'Did you have a cuddle with mummy this morning?' and Sharon nodded yes and some weight was lifted off the teacher's shoulders.

Sharon stayed on her teacher's lap right through story time and when Miss Ferdinand stood up she sat back down with the rest of the class and sang along with some energy while waiting for the end of the day and home time. Then all the other children were collected but no one came for Sharon and she went into the hall and sat beside Emma with the other fifteen children who were late being picked up.

One by one the children went until only Emma and Sharon were left alongside Ade. Mrs Welbeck had given Ade a message to say her mother had phoned to say she was delayed at the hospital. The door opened and it was Natalie with Wayne on her hip. 'I've come for Sharon and Emma,' she explained to Mrs Welbeck. 'Their mum's got terrible diarrhoea and can't get out of the house.

Mrs Welbeck let Sharon and Emma go with Natalie. As soon as they were outside Emma said, 'Where's mum?'

And Natalie said, 'She's at home,' but really Natalie could not be sure.

Bob Browning worked in the hospital laundry. He was paid extra money for handling wet laundry and extra money for handling foul laundry and extra money for working with the surgical gowns. It was not a lot extra but he also worked extra hours every Saturday morning. The money went on top of his pension for thirty-one years' service in the Army. His hair was oiled and brushed back and his shoes always immaculately polished.

He rarely spoke to anyone outside of polite greetings and read a popular newspaper at morning and afternoon breaks. After work was finished on a Friday evening or a Saturday lunchtime, he would go to a public house and stand at the bar and drink three pints of beer. Sometimes four pints and sometimes a whisky or two. Then he went home to the wife he adored.

Bob Browning started his day's work emptying two large laundry sacks and sorting through the mass of linen and the loading of it into the big eight-foot-tall washing machines. As he separated sheets from towels from clothing from pillow cases Derek Gerrard was stood in the morgue over a naked corpse with a scalpel in his hand. His eyes were fixed on the faded writing on the body's hand. There were two words side by side and underneath some numbers. The first had four letters, the second five. There were five numbers.

The words were a name, like every word was a name, like sun meant this ball of unfathomable light in the sky, like blue was the colour of the space around eight-foot-tall. Every man and every woman has this sound that is theirs and this sound in them. The most powerful thing that man has is how he can tell another man, how he can say to another, it is this or it is him.

Derek Gerrard stared at the name. It was him, Derek Gerrard, that wanted to take his human heart. It was Derek Gerrard who thought that he could, that the body would be abused and broken and he, Derek Gerrard could help himself to the human heart. The name on the body stared back at him. It was nothing special but it was a name, a human sound attached to the lump of flesh.

The sun was climbing up into the sky and the city was a grey stain spread across the river slowly making its way down to the sea. The moon was still there, a white smudge receding against a haze of blue and the planet rotated. As the horizon dipped a minute passed and another and another and the slow spinning mass in space continued utterly indifferent to the action of any man.

Each minute passed and was gone forever. Time was the rotation of a mass in space; it could not be undone, rewound or replayed. The small surgical nick on the thorax of the body could not be taken back. Now the body had a name, an identity, now the body was a human sound, it was John MacAvoy, now it was composed not just of flesh and blood of artery and organ, but of a thousand million moments when it touched or saw or was heard by an ear or loved by another on the planet as it careered through space.

Derek Gerrard threw the scalpel across the room. It tinkled against the ceramic tiles as it skidded across the floor. Now the body could and would be found. The police trawling the morgues for people reported missing would find John MacAvoy and would identify the naked corpse immediately and whoever would be informed. He took off his face mask and went and sat at his desk.

Bob Browning was pulling sheets, wet and steaming, from the barrel of the industrial washing machine. He dumped them in a wheeled laundry basket and took them over to the ironing and drying machine. Each sheet had to be pulled up and opened from corner to corner to be fed flat into the rollers that pulled it away and down over hot air and between more rollers before it was returned back to where it had been first fed in hot, flat and still steaming. Then Bob would pick it up and fold it expertly, once on the table, to add to his pile of neat crisp clean hospital sheets.

Bob knew that at home Phyllis was going to the shops for groceries and knew that on his mantelpiece there was the picture of his daughter and a picture of his son. Handling the hot steamy sheets slowly heated your hands until the flesh was inflamed on the finger tips and so dry it would crack. Bob carried on and when he got home that evening, he sat with Phyllis and watched television and occasionally would glance with pride at the photographs of their two children.

Derek Gerrard phoned Pat Driscombe in Patient Affairs. Her phone was on the answerphone. 'I have identified that unknown. Thanks. Derek Gerrard,' he said.

Dr Richard Jones stood by his office window. He had removed his jacket. He walked over to his desk and picked up the phone. 'Send Annabel in,' he said, and went and stood by the window again.

The moment the door began to open he focused himself on the entrance of the young woman. As she appeared he smiled and said, 'Annabel – do sit down,' gesturing to the upright chair on the opposite side of the desk from his.

'Good,' he said, as he settled into his chair with the desk between them. He put his hands in his lap.

'Tell me, Annabel – has it been a positive experience with my team?'

You do not get selected for fast-track schemes without

the ability to present effectively at a senior level and Annabel competently recited all the positive learning experiences she had been presented with at Dr Richard Jones' policy unit.

He sat there taking her in, looking at how her dark skirt sat across her thighs, just above her knees and looking at the buttons on her blouse and trying to discern the shape of her breasts inside the lapel of her jacket.

'Good, good,' he said, taking one hand out of his lap and picking up a pen from the desk. Rolling the pen between thumb and finger he said, 'and of course I want all the feedback and insights you can offer me.'

For a moment he took his eyes off her as if poised to make a note but as she began some highly considered remarks about the functioning of his unit, Dr Jones smiled and murmured, 'Oh, interesting.' 'Oh, really.' 'Oh good, good,' as Annabel talked with confidence and intelligence. He could see she had small breasts and he could see a small pink ornamental bow on her bra. He stood up and walked three paces away from the desk and heard her voice dip with a momentary loss of confidence. When he turned and looked at her, she continued as before.

'Good, good. That's fine,' he said, and sat back in his chair.

'Now, Annabel,' he hesitated to give the moment some gravitas.

'Could you see yourself joining the policy un t?'

Annabel spoke about how it would be a tremendous opportunity to be grasped with both hands and how hard work would be involved but how it was really exactly the sort of exciting opportunity she was looking for.

Dr Richard Jones smiled pleasantly and took in her

increased animation and watched how her cheeks flushed with excitement. She moved forward in her chair and he could see a gap between her thighs beneath her skirt.

'Excellent,' he said. 'I do so enjoy building teams. We will have to see what we can arrange for you.'

Annabel was reading this as a job offer and calculating the monthly take home pay and now, she was telling Dr Richard Jones how much she admired him and wanted to work for him.

'Good,' he said. 'You must come out to our place one day soon. I have been known to throw a rather jolly pool party.'

Annabel generated polite enthusiasm and acceptance of the invitation and Jones continued, 'Good, it can be great fun. My son Adam is generally around and some neighbours we call the Elsworthy boys, and always a few more.

'Sounds terrific,' said Annabel.

'OK, well I'll confirm a date with you tomorrow.'

As she walked out of the door Jones tried to make out the form of her underwear beneath her skirt. He looked at his watch. It was good that Yolanda was getting the help she needed. It was not sustainable to have her threatening the family's security with her attitude and with her attitude you could never tell what might be said. Disturbed people subject to psychotic episodes can end up saying anything. Not that anything could ever be proved. There was no one there.

He walked back over to the window and felt his heart pounding, dully, like background noise. He pulled the small blue pill box from his jacket pocket. He opened it and put the tablets in his mouth. There was no water left in the water jug on the tray next to the coffee cups on the shelf in front of the bookcase.

The tablets began to crumble acidic juice onto his tongue. He picked up the phone and his persona assistant answered and he said, 'Replace the drinking water in here.' and paused and sneered, 'Now,' as the dry crumbs of the pharmaceuticals began to spread around his teeth.

Looking down on the street he could see a newspaper vendor selling the evening paper and the headline about a child rapist getting life in prison. Last night on the local television news there had been one of those suicides where you really wondered what was going on. His tongue was trying to clean the crumbs of the pills from his teeth. Strangely his fist was clamped shut.

Those suicides were nearly always about money and that was not a worry for Dr Richard Jones with his income and pension. And everything was fine. It was a different era and everyone was a bit more open. You couldn't expect men of exceptional brilliance and power not to be unusual. Or just a bit kinky. Everything was fine, just needed to get poor Yolanda looked after.

Elizabeth came into the office carrying a jug of fresh water which she exchanged for the empty one on the tray. She asked, 'Anything else, Richard?'

He managed a curt, 'No fine,' and she left the room as always full of admiration for his clean white shirts and always overawed by his importance.

Yolanda looked up from the floor of the hospital cubicle and the American woman rocked back on her heels and ducked her head down and looked into her face.

'Is your family here?' she asked.

'They're waiting,' said Yolanda, and the woman peered down towards where Gwen and Adrian sat.

'Is that your mother?'

'Yep, and my brother,' said Yolanda.

The American woman looked at Yolanda. She had that way of making stylised exaggerated gestures. This time she brought her finger up and rested it on her cheek to indicate a moment of thought.

'Umm,' she said.

'Who are you?' Yolanda got up, suddenly a bit irritated by the stranger.

'I'm Rebecca,' said the American, 'I'm a volunteer here. Nothing else.'

Yolanda was deflated.

Rebecca did a theatrical peer down towards the waiting room and then a half turn to face Yolanda. 'Your father's not here?' she said, half stating and half asking.

'No,' said Yolanda.

A nurse walked past with an empty wheelchair and Rebecca took half a step into the cubicle, rolling her eyes as if she had been inconvenienced and she stepped back out with an exaggerated look behind her.

'Do you want to go onto the…' Rebecca paused as if to give the words some theatrical edge, 'psychiatric ward?'

Yolanda felt a moment's hope.

Natalie stood outside Sue's door with Sharon and Emma and Wayne in the pushchair. The bell was not working so she tapped her hand on the door with her door keys. There was no movement so she tapped again. Much harder. She waited for a few minutes. Sharon and Emma were quiet and patient. She was about to tap again when the door opened. Sue was still unwashed.

'Go inside,' she said immediately to her daughters. She looked at Natalie with pure contempt and some hatred.

Natalie felt the bad feeling and asked, 'Sue, what is it?'

Sue reinforced her face with a touch of aggression and said, 'Thanks for bringing them down but don't ever do it again.'

'Sure,' Natalie was taken aback by the malice. 'Sue – what is it?'

Natalie's friend paused and Natalie could see past her into her house, past her open door into the living room where nothing had been tided away, where nothing had been put right.

'After how you carried on last night, I don't ever want you in my house or near my kids ever again.' Sue looked at Natalie, 'Get it?' she said.

Natalie was reeling, trying to process the way things were suddenly reversed, how her friend was being so hateful towards her.

'Sue,' she said with a touch of pleading.

'Wait there,' said Sue and she went away from the door and into the living room and in to the kitchen. Nothing had been moved from the previous night.

Sue went into the kitchen cupboard and went into the money Will had left for her and pulled off a note from the wad and took it back to the door where Natalie stood.

'Thanks for picking up the kids for me, Natalie,' she said, and held out the note for Natalie while making a face that was smug and contemptuous on the surface and angry and raging underneath.

Natalie looked at the money and hesitated and Sue said with a superior knowingness, 'Take it Natalie – you've got to feed them.'

Natalie took the money and Sue gave her one more grimace of disgust before closing the door abruptly and with satisfaction.

Natalie turned the pushchair away and made her way back to her house holding the folded money in her hand. Once indoors she sat down and tried to understand why Sue had cast her out. It was easy to see that Sue was trying to blame everything that had happened on her but Natalie thought, she was already at it with Alan. The thing between her and Alan was already happening and it was Sue who had invited her around and it was Sue who had let the guys in.

Natalie put Wayne back in his pushchair and opened the door and pushed him out into the passageway. She pushed the pushchair up between the blocks of dwellings and into the road where the traffic and buses passed all day and most of the night. Natalie pushed Wayne in his pushchair into the shop on the corner of two roads and pulled out the note. She bought a card for travelling on the buses and a can of spaghetti in tomato sauce and a loaf of bread. There were two coins left afterwards.

Natalie went back to her house and put the bread on the table with the tin of spaghetti and left out one of the coins next to it. Her boys had their own keys and now there was food on the table for them when they came in. And some money for chips if they wanted it. Then she put a child's jumper over the back of the pushchair and hung her old red anorak over the handles.

Outside again she couldn't help glancing down toward

Sue's as she set out heading off the estate. As she pushed the pushchair up the ramp and out into the road, she could see Alan and Tony walking away from her and towards the shop that sold alcohol and tobacco and not much else.

At the bus stop, Natalie took Wayne out of the pushchair which she folded up. The small boy stood on his own for three minutes before beginning to whinge and cry for his mother to pick him up. She picked him up and got him looking at the cars and soon a single-decker bus could be seen approaching down the road. When it pul ed up and opened its doors Natalie was prepared with her travel pass between her teeth, the pushchair in her left hand and Wayne clamped to her hip with her right hand.

She put the pushchair between her legs for a moment and showed the driver her pass before returning it to between her teeth and sweeping the pushchair into the storage position with her left hand. Then she and Wayne sat down on a seat next to a badly-shaved elderly man. Wayne stood up on his mother's lap and looked over her shoulder at the passengers on the bus.

The bus cut through a sector of the city linking shopping streets in one location to shopping streets in another and pushing through areas of housing and through traffic systems that covered the ground in tarmac and concrete. Every four or five hundred yards the bus would pull over and the hydraulics would hiss open the doors and people would get on and people would get off.

The bus pulled up outside a large supermarket that was part of an area where people came to shop and almost everyone got off the bus. There was a gaggle of people waiting to get on and Natalie struggled to make room to fold down the pushchair. Then she did and put Wayne back into it.

Most routes ran from the outer edges in towards the middle but some ran across segments, part of a circle connecting across without going into the centre. Natalie was now looking for her second bus, the one numbered 253, that would roll through an arc across the city and would connect with the last huddle of housing that sat inside the canal that ran down the edge of the industrial area of factories and breakers yards.

The bus would rumble down what was known as murder mile, past the rows of poor shops selling fried chicken and alcohol and the garage with the bullet proof glass for the night cashiers. It would go over the round-about past the night club where feuding criminals occasionally ambushed one another and past more shops until the densely packed low-level housing took over and then you could see the road sweep around to your right and on the left an opening up of the view across some tatty grass and car parks stood three twenty-two-storey tower blocks.

Here Natalie picked up the pushchair and got off. The grass was spotted with children's disposable nappies thrown from the upper floors and the occasional burst bag of rubbish. There was a concrete ramp with handrails up to the plateau that the supporting pillars for the tower were based on. Through a set of glass doors in steel frames you reached a foyer area with access controlled through a second set of doors with a panel of numbered steel buttons set on a steel panel with the numbers of each flat engraved beside it.

Natalie pushed at the steel buttons randomly. Then an elderly black man came out of the doors and she caught hold of the door as he emerged and went in with the pushchair. There were two lifts. They were set in steel frames bedded in the cream concrete wall. One served the floors with odd numbers, and one served floors with even numbers. She pushed the button for the one with even numbers.

The lift door opened and she went in with the pushchair. Natalie pushed the button for the eighteenth floor. The lift began to go up, clanking against the sides of the shaft. Natalie looked at the thick scrawls of ink on the corrugated steel panels that made up the lift walls. Both corners of the back of the lift floor were damp and stinking of stale piss.

The winding mechanism pulled the steel box up through the shaft and juddered to a halt three hundred feet high. The doors opened with a hiss and a clatter and Natalie went out onto the landing. She looked left and there was floor to ceiling armoured glass giving a view out over the city and a belt of vertigo at the end of the landing. When she looked right it was mirrored in an architect's symmetry by another.

There were four doors each accessing a two-bedroom apartment. The first door had an iron frame and bolted onto that a security door of wrought iron bars. The second door had a heavily reinforced lock and a picture of a large dog baring its teeth and the warning, *Beware of the dog*. Natalie moved down to her right. There was a door with a *Welcome* mat outside it and two small pots of flowers, one on either side. Opposite it was a scruffy door with a rainbow sticker on it and a piece of faded ribbon held by a drawing pin.

Natalie went up to this door. There was no bell that

she could see so she pulled up the letterbox and banged it shut three times. She could hear someone inside the flat walking up to the door. Natalie stepped back a pace from the door and a young woman's voice said, 'Who is it?'

Natalie said, 'I'm looking for Maggie.'

'Hold on,' said the voice inside the flat and you could hear the security chain being engaged and the door opened three inches.

Natalie could now see a young girl of maybe sixteen years in pink dungarees, a round face and red hair standing in bare feet smiling in a naturally friendly way looking at Natalie with open curiosity.

'Mum – it's someone for you,' she shouted.

Maggie appeared walking towards her door and when the girl turned away you could see that she was pregnant and heavy but her skin was glowing on her face and on her bare arms. Below her bump her legs were strong and straight and she walked easily and relaxed.

As Maggie approached the door, approached the three-inch gap between the door and the door frame she too smiled as she looked at Natalie.

'Yes,' she said.

'I'm a friend of Sue's,' said Natalie.

A shadow of doubt passed Maggie's face, a moment of suspicion, of caution. Her hand rested on the security chain. She looked at Natalie more closely and glanced at the pushchair.

'I don't want anything,' said Natalie.

'What is it?' asked Maggie.

'She is in a bit of trouble,' said Natalie.

Maggie released the security chain and said, 'Come in for a minute.'

The undertakers parked their dark grey windowless van by the delivery ramp at the rear of the hospital. It was called the service entrance. They were signed in by the duty manager and wheeled a coffin down the corridor past the kitchens, past the laundry, past maintenance to the double doors of the morgue. They loaded a body from the fridges into the coffin and wheeled the coffin on its special trolley back out to the ramp. Once the coffin was in the back of the windowless van, they could drive it to the undertaker's premises to leave the coffin in the chapel of rest.

Derek Gerrard struggled to get John's body back into a shroud but then could store him in the recently vacated space in the fridges that hummed all day and night. He sat down at his desk, his flesh hanging flaccid off his bones. The sweat dried on his skin and dried into the hospital greens. He sat and did nothing.

Pat Driscombe came into work and was surprised to hear the message from the morgue porter. A little exclamation left her lips and she made a note on the sheet of paper where she wrote out her daily list of jobs to complete. It said, *Confirm ID of unknown. Pauper?* as it was her experience that if no one wanted the body in the first few days it would eventually be buried by the local authority, and the costs of the funeral met by the local authority and it would still be referred to by all the parties involved as a pauper's funeral.

Upstairs on the ward where Staff Nurse Lucerne had begun her day's work a groan of pain span down between the beds breaking into every head with its volume and extended length. Fear floated across the eyes of the young porter and Lucerne walked briskly towards the noise. As the groan quietened down another erupted and was gone and then a long low moan started.

Lucerne pulled back the curtain around the bed and saw an old man sat in a chair in pyjamas with no one near him and with his body making no movement. His head had fallen forward on his chest and one arm dangled unmoving down his side while the other lay inert on his lap.

Another low moaning groan came from him and Lucerne gently lifted his head and propped it against the side of the chair with two pillows. A cleaner stood staring at her from across the room with fear stamped across her face. Lucerne put her hands behind the man's knees and pulled him forward in his chair trying to get him sat straighter. Another nurse appeared at Lucerne's side and the body let out another moan, quieter than before.

'It's OK,' said Lucerne 'I don't think its pain; it's just the brain decaying.'

The other nurse looked in the man's eyes and there was no sign of any reaction, of any function, of any spark of life. She reached for a tissue on the bedside cabinet and wiped a long string of saliva off his chin.

'That's giving me the creeps,' said the young porter to his older colleague. They were sat in a very small room at the entrance to the ward.

'Dreadful. I know dreadful,' said the other man. 'It don't mean anything – just random – the brain is melting down.' He looked at the younger man with a touch of concern. 'Not nice though – and not nice for the others and frightens visitors.'

'Um,' the porter acknowledged.

'Not as bad as psychiatric anyway,' said the older man.

'That really does give you the shivers.'

'Um,' said the other man.

A single magpie flew across the sky from a large building onto a perch on a thin branch at the top of a tree. A pair of pigeons flapped and glided away and a breeze blew through the leaves. The magpie looked out over the city with its glossy black eyes and crawked twice. A magpie alone looking out over acres of housing, but seeing its own different city of trees and gardens and roofs. It looked down on everything and saw the ground as man would see the sky.

The bird shifted its feet and its head flicked this way and that way looking for its partner. A monogamous magpie coupled for life alone and searching. Always searching and calling. If you see one alone it is like a curse, one for sorrow. One for sorrow and for every time you look to count two for joy there is the haunting shadow of the one alone, sorrow and always for everyone sorrow.

The bird flew away, its black shining and its white matt and its long tail launching across the space between tree tops. It looked and called and looked and called and flew another short hop to edge guttering on a five-storey office block. Below only a man disengaged from everyday bustle could look up, could see, for all to see one for sorrow.

Rebecca was beautiful. Yolanda could see that the American woman held an internal elegance grafted onto her firm lithe figure and cheek-boned pretty face. She had thick curled blonde hair bobbed short. Her black polo neck jumper showed off her straight shoulders and back. She stood in the doorway of a cubicle in the emergency department of the hospital. Yolanda sat there quietly waiting to be taken to the psychiatric ward.

Rebecca took just half a step forward. She spoke firmly 'What's your name?'

Quietly she heard the woman say, 'Yolanda.'

Rebecca took the step back and spoke again, casually and relaxed. 'So Yolanda, you don't want to go to the psychiatric ward?'

Yolanda looked at the floor and moved her head from side to side.

'Hey,' said Rebecca and again, 'Hey,' and Yolanda looked up and Rebecca said, 'Do you want to go to…'

And Yolanda looked down quickly and said quietly in a voice with hardly any strength, 'No,' and there was a moment when the silence was thick between the figure sat forward on the chair looking at the floor and the glamorous American standing six feet away. Yolanda looked from the floor and looked at Rebecca and Yolanda's face was grey and tired and the lines around her mouth and eyes were deep and her eyelids heavy and her eyes not quite focused. Her lips barely opened as she tried to smile.

Rebecca saw Yolanda's face come up at her and saw all the fatigue and stress and exhaustion. She saw the woman's spirit grey and flat and pummelled and saw all the brokenness and saw the hollow helplessness in the weak and fading smile. Rebecca turned away, turned her back and looked out into the corridor. She set her chin and clenched her teeth. The wave of pity, of understanding, flashed through her and glanced tears into her eyes. She took a step away from the door and clenched her two fists at her sides and forced composure and lightness into every atom of her body, into every inch of her appearance. Rebecca turned back to face Yolanda.

'Kay,' Rebecca said, lightly abbreviating OK. She half-turned and put her finger to her chin in her thinking pose 'Umm, Kay,' she repeated, and then straightened up as if suddenly inspired and stepped back into the corridor and peered down into the waiting room before stepping back into the cubicle and taking another step in towards Yolanda. She spoke lightly.

'Hey, Yolanda, do you think your family is the problem here?'

Yolanda sat up and back on the chair. She held her head up and pushed her hips forward a bit. She nodded. The weak smile played on her lips.

'Uh-oh,' said Rebecca, and she distractedly pulled a piece of fluff off her dark wool jumper. Rebecca glanced at Yolanda for a tiny moment taking in her face and eyes. She spun around as if to leave and then turned back as if having an unexpected afterthought causing her surprise.

'And your father, part of it as well?'

Yolanda's left eyelid closed and the remnants of the attempted smile disappeared and she nodded.

'Kay,' said Rebecca. 'You stay here honey, I am going to use the phone,' and the glamorous American took a parting look at Yolanda before executing a spin on her heels and walking out of the cubicle and turning left towards the nurses' station.

Yolanda sat still on her chair.

Emma and Sharon sat on the settee eating beans on toast.

Sue had picked up the ashtrays and put them in the kitchen. She had not used the hoover or tidied the room. The girls were watching a cartoon and Sue told them, 'I am just going round to the shop – I'll get you ice cream,' and she went out of her door walking quickly and breaking into a jogging run through the walkway between the blocks.

She bought a bottle of wine and a small packet of cigarettes and two large ice creams for Emma and Sharon. As she turned back onto the estate, she heard a male voice shout, 'Sue,' and she broke into a slow run with her key in one hand and the plastic bag with the shopping in the other. She didn't look around or look back in the direction of the voice and got herself to her front door and got the door open before hearing a second, 'Sue,' and as she stepped into her house she thought she could hear male voices laughing before she shut the door quickly and hard.

In her kitchen she poured herself a glass of wine and then went and collected the children's dirty plates and gave them their ice creams. The cartoon was still squeaking on the television. Emma drew her legs up on the settee and started on her ice cream and said loudly as Sue was returning to the kitchen, 'Mum – have you done the washing?'

Sue said, 'No, I'll do some in a minute,' and finished the first glass of wine.

Outside by the ramp out of the estate two glossy black crows were picking over the carcass of a cooked chicken that had fallen from the rubbish bins as they were being emptied. Two black beaks pecked at the ribcage and pulled at the remnants of flesh and fat around the legs and wings. The carcass shifted along on the ground as it was tugged by first one crow and then the other.

Up on the eighteenth floor Natalie followed Maggie into her living room. Two sides of the room had windows running the width of the walls from waist height to the ceiling. The room was small with the furniture against the back two walls facing the windows. The view was out over an industrial district of randomly collated factory units and a scrapyard with openings for a lorry park and cars to be left between white lines outside low office blocks.

There was a small table and two chairs against one window. It was a table where Maggie would sit with her daughter Rose and look out over the messy outer limits of the city and talk about what to do. Wayne had dozed off in the pushchair and Maggie offered Natalie a cup of tea. Rose bent down in front of the pushchair and looked at Wayne saying, 'Aah he's lovely,' and asking, 'How old is he?'

And Natalie replied and asked, 'When are you due?' and Rose told her.

Maggie brought in two cups of tea and sat with Natalie at the table. Rose sat on an armchair looking at a magazine pushing the pushchair forwards and backwards with her foot.

'So what is it?' said Maggie as she sat down.

Natalie put her hand around the mug of hot tea and was unable to speak about Sue. Sue's sister, Maggie, had the same close likenesses. In profile you see the shape of Sue's face and they had the same skin tone and the same hair. But Sue was slim and walked and moved with an apparent energy whereas Maggie was broad hipped and heavy legged and gave a deliberate air to her every move. Sue had always been the girl pushing forward, and Maggie had always been the one catching life as it comes.

Maggie's furniture and decoration was worn and she had covered the split fabric and multiple stains on the sofa and armchair with a combination of different loose blankets and throws. She lived with Rose and was five years older than Sue, twice her daughter's age.

Natalie took in the comfortable warmth of Maggie's room and wanted to say nothing about Sue, not to have to bring anxiety and distress into the house. She felt Maggie looking at her and she looked over at Rose sitting comfortably and rocking the pushchair and Natalie looked away and out the window at the clouds shifting across a wide sky over all the grey and brown blocks of habitations of the city as far as you could see.

Natalie found herself staring into her tea and a flustered heat rising in her cheeks. She couldn't think of what word to say or what sentence to begin with to start to tell even one a small part of what she wanted to say. Maggie sat down opposite her and looked at Natalie who kept her eyes on her tea and on the table.

Maggie let a moment pass but kept her gaze on Natalie and said, 'Well you better tell me what's going on.'

Natalie grappled with her shame, with an image of her enthusiasm for some excitement and with her memory of what she had done and been doing. She struggled to escape from those recalls, to think what it was that has made her come over to this location halfway up to the sky. It was not because of those moments of her carnal wantonness, not because of Sue's, it was not about what they had done.

Natalie glanced out the window and her eyes passed over Maggie's face. She looked back down at the table.

'She's not minding the girls,' she said.

Maggie's face set hard and she looked at Natalie and over at Wayne. Her voice had a different tone. It was level and flat, so flat that it was harsh.

'What do you mean by that?'

Natalie was heavy on her chair. Her hands played with her mug of tea and she kept her gaze down. She could feel Maggie's rage that she should come and say that her sister was not looking after her children. That she was not a mother.

Natalie tried to pull it back, 'She's a lovely mum, Maggie, but something happened. She forgot them at school.'

Maggie was alert with her anger. 'What's happened?'

Natalie tried to look up to meet Maggie's gaze but saw an accusing smirk on her face and blushed with shame and her head dropped lower. Maggie's voice was still level.

'What have you been up to?'

Natalie felt her own disgrace but she was not going to let this woman judge her and she was not going to judge this woman or her sister nor was anyone going to set them-selves above her and Wayne and her boys. Anger flashed into Natalie and she gathered back the tears she had felt and stood up and looked to reach for the pushchair.

Her voice was breaking. 'Look – she needs a hand, go and see her.'

Natalie was getting to the handles to manoeuvre the pushchair out of the living room.

Maggie stood up slowly. 'Have you got something to tell me?'

Natalie was trying to get into the hallway that led to the door. She opened the front door and pushed Wayne out. Maggie walked towards her. Natalie was out of Maggie's house and on the landing.

Now the tears were in her eyes and every movement was hesitant and upset.

Maggie said, 'Natalie?'

And Natalie said, 'You have to go to see her.'

Natalie's thumb was pressing the button for the lift and you could hear the mechanism moving up the metal box. Natalie stood determinedly staring at the lift doors and heard Maggie pull shut her front door. She pushed Wayne into the lift and wiped a tear from her cheek.

At the bus stop she stood waiting with her child asleep over her shoulder and the pushchair ready in her left hand. On the bus she let the child sleep on her lap and stared out of the window her face set. She looked down at her flat shoes with the seam split by her left little toe and looked at where her thighs were rubbing through the material of her leggings.

Maggie's accusations: *What have you been up to? What do you mean by that*? replayed as the bus ground on stopping and starting, making its way back down murder mile past shops and houses and more shops and traffic intersections. Natalie sat still absorbing the bumps and stops and braking, thinking, not of Maggie, not of Sue and not of Wayne but of Emma and Sharon.

The bus rocked on and Natalie let an angry curse build up inside. It was, *Yeah, fuck you, Maggie, for even trying to point the finger at me and fuck you, Sue, for your nastiness – yeah fuck you, Sue, for thinking you were so much better with all your fancy fucking furniture and everything you ever wanted – yeah fuck you, bitch*, but it crumbled when she thought of the girls, of their shattered home and busted mother.

Wayne only half woke up when she had to change buses and as Natalie closed in on her home territory her anxiety eased. Maggie would have to come over. She would have to. Her son's head was warm on her breast and Natalie pushed out her feet in front of her. She could see a cluster of broken veins in the arch of her foot and she could see the city's grime smudged around her ankles. On her left hand she wore three cheap rings. The sunlight caught the window of the bus and mirrored back a portrait of her long dark hair, of the child asleep and of her eyes closing for only moments between the bus's jolts.

The city thins out away from the centre. There is more green and the splotches of grey civilisation become more spread out. The train line runs from the city centre to the sea connecting through town after town running past fields and woods and fields throwing up square acres of yellow flowers they call rape. Roads carry cars speeding between the towns and cars sometimes smash into lorries and sometimes run off the road and teenagers on the brink of their life die there, their laughter left forever hanging.

Others flock to the city drawn likes moths to the bulb. There is a migration of the young into the great chaotic mass and a trickle of people. Of couples, of young families out to the ordered suburbs. Some flock to the city from far off continents and some come in from no further than a daily commute. All the towns and cities send some down to the capital, there is always someone else from your place somewhere in the city.

Coming into the city the train threads through stations

and fields and another station then more fields. Then that stops and it is all housing then housing and factories crowding in on the railway. And then finally the city crawls over the railway and the train swings into its terminus and delivers its load and the doors open and people pour out. Thousands and thousands every day and in amongst those thousands the migrants from all corners.

You could see the graveyard from the train. You could see the sudden opening out of acre and acre of paths between grass split by stone tablets stuck in the ground. In the corner of that graveyard you could see a yellow mechanical excavator, its scoop down on the ground. There are some men standing there, maybe five maybe seven.

A grey van drives down the path towards the yellow excavator. The driver gets out and walks past the excavator and toward a large square hole in the ground. He looks down into it. He goes back to the van. Another man is walking towards the van and the excavator and the small group standing turn. This person is wearing a big robe and holding a book. He stands beside the square hole.

The back door of the van is opened by the driver. Two other men get out of the front seat and go to the rear of the van. They pull out a coffin and two men hold it by the front handles and one holds it up, by its tail. They walk over to the square hole. The men who are standing around move towards the hole.

The driver of the van returns to the vehicle and comes back carrying two webbing straps. These are threaded through the coffin handles.

The man in the robe opens his book. The two men from the front of the van lift up the coffin by the webbing straps and straining against the weight lower it down.

Down in the hole there are four coffins lying side by side. These four coffins lie across four coffins below them. The coffin is lowered down and is the first coffin of the third layer. The man in the robe is reading from his book with mumbled quiet words. One of the men watching puts out a cigarette and treads on it. The city is burying its dead.

The men from the van drop one end of their webbing straps and recover them by hauling up on the other end. They go back to their vehicle and drive off. The man in the long robe mumbles a prayer and says amen. He looks around for a moment. None of the men gathered there offers an amen. He turns away and walks through the stones on the black tarmac path.

Another of the men lights a cigarette and then another. They are standing together uncertain but all familiar. Someone says, 'He would have expected us to have a drink,' There is a quiet half chuckle. 'Where are we going?' 'It has to be The Cricketers,' says someone else.

The first two men turn away and start walking away and another follows. A tall man stares down into the hole observing how the coffins are stacked. Beside him is another man, shorter and muscular. For a moment they take in the neat tidy stack and the tall man lets out a breath and looks at his friend, 'Sort of cosy though,' and the friend grins although his face is creased and his eyes are moist.

They too walk away and a cloud crosses the sky and takes the heat off the sun and throws a shadow carelessly across the city. Then the cloud shifts and the sun plays strands of light through thick broken edges and a breeze touches the faces of the friends as they walk away. They make for the ornate iron gates passing through all the stones carrying notifications of lives spent and gone. The numbers and names and all the multiples of family, of mum and wife and child all recorded on these tablets. Some were askew and almost fallen and some fresh and new and some dark and some light.

They made the gates and another van came in and headed for the yellow excavator and the square hole. Then they stood outside as a black hearse with a coffin bedecked with flowers came through the gates at the head of a procession of dark cars filled with family and friends. And then they made their way out onto the busy city street and walked slowly towards the bus stop.

Pat Driscombe phones down to the mortuary. Derek Gerrard picks up the phone. She says 'Hi, It's Pat. Did they take that one for the pauper's this morning?'

'Yes,' says the morgue porter.

'Thank you,' says Pat Driscombe. She puts down the phone.

John has been buried.

A man up in space, in tubes of metal bolted together, floating through the eternal darkness stares down at earth, at all the wonder of life. From his cocoon of man's greatest technology, he sees the wonder of the planet, everything beautiful, and is forever changed. They are all changed when they come back from up there, all sighted with the beauty of it, blown apart with the marvel of what is down there.

Down there below the stream of clouds and between the swirls of seas are the lands and some are yellow or brown and some are green. The green land we see has the grey spreading city cut by the river and then running out more green between suburbs and beyond the suburbs more green. Trees and grassland and acres of crops of wheat and barley for bread, for beer, for everything and trees bearing fruit.

Square upon square of green bordered by darker lines of hedges and lines and specks that are yards and houses. Trees gathered near streams and brooks and cows and sheep grazing. Then here and there the squares of blazing yellow, acre and square acre of yellow blocked into the landscape. They call it rape.

Rape like the children drunk and drugged and taken from restaurant to restaurant, like the broken body of a girl child in a suitcase obliterated by her father and uncles raping her for honour, like a pimp seasoning a whore, like all that and more than you can hear. You cannot see it all, you cannot ask, never ask. There is one magpie for sorrow, sure, and seven for a story never to be told.

The mad guy in the cubicle next to Yolanda was still playing with the light switch. Rebecca appeared again in front of Yolanda. 'Hi,' she said, to get her attention.

Yolanda looked up and saw the American woman's smooth skin and accurately applied bright lipstick. Rebecca smiled gently as if proudly presenting her homework to a teacher.

'I'm sort of done!' She said, 'That doctor is going to come back and send you home.'

Yolanda looked at her trying to take it in and looked away trying to understand.

Rebecca sensed she needed to confirm it again. 'The doctor will come back. They might give you some pills to take away. But you're not going...' she hesitated as if there was an indelicate unmentionable, 'into any ward,' she finished.

Yolanda looked at her in the face and Rebecca just raised her arm a bit and nodded and Yolanda knew it was safe and trusted and there was a shy smile on the American's lips.

Yolanda breathed and felt something lift and wanted to ask questions but didn't want to question or shift the new reality so said.

'Where are you from?'

'America,' said Rebecca.

'Oh I got that,' said Yolanda, 'but where?'

'California,' said the blonde American.

'Really?' said Yolanda.

'Yep – Los Angeles,' said Rebecca.

Yolanda looked away suddenly studying the painted hospital wall. In her head was the hopeless chorus, always repeating, always had repeated, always connecting two phrases so Yolanda had never heard the words without the other things in her head, it always was, 'Los Angeles, City of Angels.'

She turned back and Rebecca was still stood there and Yolanda wanted to know so much but the American was looking away down the corridor distracted as if time was running out.

'OK. She's coming down,' said Rebecca looking back at Yolanda, 'You just accept the pills and get yourself home. OK?'

Yolanda felt a certain urgency in the instruction so

nodded and said, 'Of course.'

'Good,' said Rebecca.

'One thing though,' said Yolanda.

A moment's irritation passed Rebecca's face but she refocused and responded, 'Yes.'

'How did you know?'

Rebecca looked at Yolanda. A hardness, an unmoving of any muscle, crossed her face. A closing down of any giving was suddenly there.

'Personal experience,' she said, and forced a grin and raised her left hand a bit before she turned away, looked left down the corridor. Wheeled away right and was gone.

As Yolanda stood up to see her go Dr Clare appeared in the doorway holding a prescription in her hand.

'Oh good,' she said. 'I've spoken with a colleague and we think perhaps...'

Yolanda followed the doctor out into the waiting room and the doctor held out the prescription which Acrian took. Dr Clare spoke with Gwen briefly and then Yolanda followed her mother and brother out of the door of the institution, out of the enormous concrete multi-storeyed block, out into the blazing sun and the summer warmth and a breeze blowing down the city streets and she looked at the blue sky between the buildings. Adrian went back inside to cash the bit of paper for a bottle of pills and Gwen found herself a bench to sit on. Yolanda stretched her arms up towards the sky and breathed.

'You better come back with us,' said Gwen.

'Okay,' said Yolanda.

Adrian came out with a paper bag and inside that was a plastic container of pills and Yolanda and her mother and brother made their way home to the suburbs. As the train rocked across green fields Yolanda looked at Adrian and he looked up. She said, 'I'm looking forward to meeting your girlfriend.' Adrian smiled thinly.

Back in the family house Gwen poured herself a large glass of red wine and started preparing food. Adrian went out to the garage. Yolanda watched television. It was two hours before Dr Richard Jones got home. The paper bag with the pills was on the kitchen table.

On the television a popular singing contest was taking place. Yolanda lay on the couch with knees drawn up. When her father came into the room, she followed him with her eyes but did not shift her body. He sat down in an armchair.

'They've given you very strong anti-psychotic drugs. It's obvious they are really worried about you, Yolanda.'

She looked at her father. He went on, 'You are a very unstable person; your mother is at her wits' end with worry.'

Yolanda sat up on the couch and looked at Dr Richard Jones, her father. Rebecca knew. She knew immediately. Rebecca has phoned someone. So they knew as well. Someone else knew. It wasn't just something in Yolanda's mind now. She wasn't locked up in a psychiatric ward.

She looked at her father. He got up and left the room. Yolanda lay back down and watched the talent show on the television.

All day the sun beat down into the concrete and bricks of the city. Buildings soaked up the energy and then the night came and lights went on and slowly the heat ebbed out. Then the sky lightened as the chill began to override everything and then it lightened more and golden rays bounced refracted off clouds into the atmosphere. The chill weakened and was dispersed and up came the blazing orb and another day was gifted. Light fought away the shadows.

Sue had slept downstairs. She had fallen asleep late after nearly two bottles of wine. The girls had come down in the morning. She shouted at them to go back upstairs. Then she sat on the sofa with her head in her hands. She shouted upstairs, 'You're having a play day at home. No school.'

Emma started crying quietly. Sue went into the kitchen. There was bread in the cupboard and no milk and no cereal. She pulled out some money and shouted upstairs. 'Stop that noise – I'm just going to the shop.'

Sue opened the door and looked both ways. There was no sign of anyone. She darted out of her door and half ran to the shop. As well as the milk and cereal and bread she bought eggs and beans and a newspaper and then a large pack of frozen chips and fish fingers from the fridge. She also picked up some crisps and sweets and fizzy drinks. The man in the shop put the stuff in a bag for her.

'Do you want cigarettes?' he said.

'Oh yeah,' said Sue, and he pulled down the pack and put them in the bag with the shopping.

The shop man smiled a friendly smile and gestured towards the shelves with alcohol and said, 'Anything else you want?'

Sue thought it would save her coming out again later so added a bottle of wine to her shopping. She looked both ways out of the shop door before stepping out into the morning air.

Back indoors she put the shopping in the kitchen and went upstairs. Emma was lying on her bed tears all over her face. She went to her and said, 'Come here,' and cuddled her and explained, 'We are all having a lovely day together today. You will be back at school tomorrow.'

Emma settled down and accepted her mother's promise and Sue went into her and Will's unslept bedroom and picked up her hairbrush and brushed her hair. She went past the girls' room and announced again, 'We're really going to have a lovely day today,' and she went downstairs.

At school Sharon and Emma were marked absent with a large A in the registers and Miss Smith sighed heavily and tried to get on with her day. The parents that had congregated around the school gate began to walk away, the little crowd moving out in different directions.

The police helicopter was hovering loud over a location half a mile away and a large passenger jet was banking right to pick up the course for its final approach. The drone of the traffic down the main road was continuous and a small motorbike with a blown exhaust could be heard from somewhere nearby. The children inside the school settled down at their tables.

Sue gave the girls hot toast and let them have the television on. She opened the door that opened out onto the back yard and fresh air came into the room. After the girls had finished eating their toast, she gave them a fizzy drink each.

With the backdoor open you could hear other voices from the estate and hear the slamming doors and the starting and stopping of cars. Sue stood by the door drinking tea and smoking a cigarette. She did not step out into the yard, not even one foot. Then she heard male voices talking and laughing. She hurriedly threw down her cigarette and quickly shut the door.

She tried to read the newspaper. Emma turned off the television. Sharon tried to sit on her mother's lap. Emma stood up and said, 'Mum, when is daddy coming back?'

Sue said, 'Next week.'

And Sharon said, 'Will he have presents?'

And Sue said, 'Of course,' and Emma started crying and sat down next to Sue. Then Sharon started crying as well and after a couple of minutes, Sue said, 'Come on, that will do – turn it off now.'

She got up and went into the kitchen, flustered before a shot of anger had her voice raised, 'That will do. Stop it now.'

And Sharon was sobbing but Emma said, 'It wouldn't be like that if Daddy was here.'

And Sue couldn't help herself but say to her daughter, 'Like what, like what?' and the child's small challenge had pitched Sue into a shouting, raging state, 'Like what? What do you mean? Tell me what you mean?' and Emma shrunk back in her chair and Sue said, 'You don't know anything, you don't know anything. What do you mean? Don't think you can talk to me like that.' She turned away and back into the kitchen and was muttering under her breath, 'Little bitch, what is she saying, little bitch.'

The children sat on the settee cowed and still. Sue went to the back door and opened it and lit a cigarette. Her hand was shaking and there were tears in her eyes. She could hear some male voices from somewhere and some-one was playing electronic music badly. A tiny black crow flew heavily over the backyards and headed for the tree at the top of the ramp. It was hot again. Sue puffed and looked back into her living room. She still hadn't cleaned up. The girls went and sat on the settee where… where she had been sleeping.

'You two go and play on the swings,' she said to her daughters.

Natalie looked out of her kitchen window. The window overlooked the walkway between the blocks. Away to her right on the opposite side she could see Sue's front door. To her left, where the blocks finished, she could see the open patch of grass with a swing made from a car tyre mounted on chains and attached to a metal frame. In the evenings children who were allowed to play out would gather there. Some boys would be on bikes and sometimes girls would have dolls in play pushchairs. It would be a busy place during school holidays and weekends and summer evenings.

Natalie went into her living room and saw Wayne was still asleep on the couch. She picked up two dirty plates and her mug that she drank tea from and went back into the kitchen. She looked out the window.

Sharon was sat on the swing and Emma was standing beside her holding onto the chain. The swing was not moving. Natalie ran the water in her sink and rinsed off her plates and mug. She put on the kettle. She could only see the swing by standing in front of her sink and leaning forward a bit.

Natalie poured boiling water from the kettle onto a teabag in her mug. She watched the girls. Emma looked like she had been crying. Both were dressed in leggings and a T-shirt and trainers. Sharon began to kick the swing into action and Emma tried to stop it by holding onto the chain. There was an animated exchange between the girls and then Emma let go of the chain and went behind the swing and began to push her sister.

Natalie sipped her tea. Sue never kept her girls off school. Never. Sharon and Emma were never allowed to play out with all the rest of the kids around the swing. The swing was flying through the air and Sharon was yelping when Emma pushed it higher. Natalie leaned forward over the sink and looked to her right. She could see Sue's front door. It was shut. She looked left and saw Emma slowing down the swing and then swapping places with Sharon. Then it was Emma flying through the air and Sharon who was pushing.

Natalie was still looking out the window when Ben walked past. She took two steps back into the shade of her kitchen and then two steps forward to watch his back as he sauntered towards Sue's. He passed her door but stopped three yards past it and pressed the bell of her next-door neighbour, the home where Alan lived. Alan came out of there and the two young men walked off in the other direction.

Natalie looked to her left and Emma and Sharon were still playing on the swing. It was noon already and the heat of the day was building. Wayne stirred and moaned and Natalie went to him.

Sue opened her back door and smoked another cigarette. She wanted to tidy the place up while the girls were out. She wanted to get it back how it was. Then she heard a man's laughter and shut the door. She picked up the hoover and plugged it in. It would only take ten minutes.

Sue went into her kitchen. She had put the shopping away in the fridge and the cupboard but she had not washed up or wiped down or emptied the rubbish or cleared away the bottles and ashtrays, but it would only take a few minutes. She put the kettle on to make tea. Then she went to the fridge and took out the bottle of wine and poured a glass. She sipped at the cold white wine and looked around. She could sort it out. It wouldn't take long.

Natalie put Wayne in the pushchair and walked past Emma and Sharon playing on the swing. She said hello and Sharon said hello back. Emma said nothing. Natalie went to the post office and cashed her child benefit and bought chicken pieces and oven chips and a box of teabags and a bag of sugar. As she walked back onto the estate, she saw Emma and Sharon moving back to their house and going inside.

The bus stopped opposite the garage on murder mile. Two men got off and walked away down the side road. They walked past the entrance to a large estate of red brick tenement blocks and along past two-storey houses, some with rubbish in their small front gardens, some tidy and some falling into disrepair. The road curved and there was a small grocery store opposite a builder's supply yard and a funeral director. Then on the corner was a rundown public house, its livery of red and cream was tatty, the windows showing grubby curtains and the paint on the sign board above the door peeling. It was called 'The Cricketers.'

Inside Lucy sat at the corner table opposite the door, and opposite the two doors in the other corner marked Ladies and Gentlemen. Michael was behind the bar and was serving pints of bright cold light lager beer to three young men in dark clothes. They got their beer and went and sat with Lucy. There was a pause and then a beer glass was raised and someone said, 'To Isaiah,' and the beer glasses were raised, and Lucy raised her glass of whisky and Coca-Cola, and glasses were clinked together and a couple of voices said, 'Isaiah.'

There was a moment of quiet and then there was a tapping on the window beside the door. A firm tap tap on the glass window. One of the young men chuckled. Michael looked over from behind the bar.

'That's probably him,' said someone, and there were a couple of short laughs and Lucy almost giggled.

Michael went over to the door and let in the two friends, Paul and Mark. They looked over at the group in the corner and nodded greetings before going to the bar and getting drinks. Then they went and joined the others around a big table – there was no one else there

'You didn't make it,' said Paul, addressing Lucy.

'Did you see me there?' asked Lucy.

'No,' Paul continued looking to excuse himself, 'but you did say you'd turn up last night.'

'Well I didn't wake up – and I'm here now,' said Lucy with a defensive frailty that Paul felt immediately.

He looked at Lucy and took in her face covered in white foundation and eyes made up with fine dark lines of mascara and dyed black hair, long and spiked and he raised his glass and smiled, 'Cheers,' he said.

Lucy smiled back and looked away.

Mark when up to the wall mounted jukebox and began selecting a tune. Dan shouted out, 'He liked The Who,' and someone said, *'My Generation,'* and loud rock chords played across the small bar. There was a pause when the tune ended and a pausing silence before the next song started. Then there was a quiet guitar picking.

Someone recognised it, and said, 'That's a bit bloody obvious,' and they then sat there as *Stairway to Heaven* played on the jukebox of a small bar with six people sat in a corner remembering their friend.

Outside a wind from the south blew warm down the road pushing dust and dirt and bits of paper into odd corners and against kerbs and walls. Flies buzzed around food waste at the back of the restaurants and across the city men fought rats with poison and traps. In places the sewage system was blocked with congealed lumps of animal fat drifting into dams across its pipes. There are people to pick up the carcasses of dead animals; there are people to bury the dead. The city goes on. Always on.

In the hospital Staff Nurse Lucerne takes the lift up to the ward. She does not get out at level 2 where the theatres are. There they put people to sleep and enter the body and take out stones and open up blockages and give back life to many who would have died. Doctors gather under the glare of the brightest lights and cut open abdomens and straighten out limbs and pull babies from wombs and stand with blood on their gloved hands doing that day after day. They cannot save everyone.

The planet circles on through days, weeks, months, years, centuries, many lifetimes and up on the ward Lucerne sits and holds hands with Patrick and lets him cry like a child, like a boy lost in a war and lets him sob until he can cry no more. Then he can turn away and sleep and his family can visit and now his tears are gone.

Out in the city squirrels take over any gathering of trees and mice run through old wooden floored buildings. Flocks of greasy starlings gather on buildings and pestilent pigeons are everywhere looking for scraps. People rush here and there following patterns and routines assuming their actions have more significance than the chemically instructed insects.

'He wasn't really called Isaiah,' said Mick.

'No,' said Paul.

'His name was John,' said Lucy. 'He was John.'

The train bore Yolanda back into the city. She walked through the crowds in the station and walked out into the city light. A bus took her away from the inner core, just a mile or two north and the plane trees begun to appear at the side the roads. Trees hanging heavy, summer boughs laden with leaves over the tarmac. Cars following buses, following vans and lorries and motorbikes around the city, around the roads, sometimes lined with trees and sometimes not.

In her home Yolanda phoned work and friends and went to the bathroom and checked her knickers were still clear and looked hard at herself in the mirror and turned away quickly. Then she went down the stairs and out the door into the street and past the shops and past the station where people flooded up from the underground railway and headed up into the market.

She moved past the shops with open fronts and blaring music that stocked the latest shoes or jackets or T-shirts, and past the stalls and past the door to backrooms offering to tattoo paint under your skin or to push metal loops through your flesh. There were lurid luminous plastic clothes and woven wools and cottons and thumping electronic music and pipes playing meditative loops.

Yolanda walked through the mostly young people taking in all the different shapes of their limbs and necks and heads and all their different ways of dressing and ways of cutting their hair. It was a carnival of humanity with some dressed in black with dark patterns on their skin and others wearing reds and yellows and greens and here and there someone sported pink-dyed hair or a bright white chemical shock standing up from their head. Music blared out from shops and stalls and groups of young men and women gathered on a bridge talking and smoking and passing around a bottle of drink.

She walked on to where the stalls offered food, past food from India from China from South America from Europe and walked on until the market crowds thinned out and the shops were the normal collection of food shops and clothing outlets. Now Yolanda's eye was caught by every woman carrying or pushing a small child, by every babe in arms or in a buggy.

In the supermarket she watched every mother and every child and watched the mother with the smallest children and passed close by the babies and stole close looks at their sleeping faces. Yolanda looked at the buggies and pushchairs and the clothes the little ones wore and the bags the mothers carried and walked through the aisles of food indifferent to all that but with her head rioting with all the changes to come.

She walked out of the supermarket with nothing and

crossed the road to a large bookshop next to the electrical shop that sold televisions and computers. Yolanda walked past the shelves of fiction and biography and went down the stairs where the basement sprawled out with all the minority interests. It was quiet and she walked her way around the shelves methodically looking at first one title then another.

Dr Richard Jones was in his office and found himself clenching and unclenching his left hand. Without doubt, he thought, his blood pressure was playing up again and he took a tablet from the little box. He found himself tuning into his own breathing and found himself feeling a touch of breathlessness. He walked over to the big window. It was over twenty years since he had more than a single glass of wine. That's how long he had been in complete control.

Yolanda came up from the basement carrying three books. She queued at the cash till and paid for them and then she went out into the light and walked slowly home through the everyday people shopping for their everyday lives. People walked in front and behind her and walked past her and there were mothers and fathers and children. A bus pulled up and disgorged its passengers onto the pavement and Yolanda pushed through the crown bumping shoulders with a woman and exchanging a quick, 'Sorry,' before carrying on up the road.

'Aaah – Annabel, good to see you,' said Dr Richard Jones to

the young woman with a touch of fake surprise as she entered his office. 'Sit down,' he said as he indicated the chair. He said down opposite her, behind his desk.

'I have a special project for you,' he said. Annabel looked at him and felt the same sense of unease that had been playing on her mind since their last meeting.

'Oh good,' she said but her voice was empty of enthusiasm. She didn't like this man.

'Yes – I will have to brief you about it – but I have meetings all day.'

Jones was continuing when Annabel stood up suddenly. Her eyes were full of tears and her face was red. Words burst out of her. 'No sorry, I'm not interested. I'm leaving,' and she walked quickly to the door, it was almost a run. The door shut behind her and she was gone.

Jones walked to the window, his left fist clenched. He had to write Annabel's assessment and he was already constructing the sentences, 'Unable to take instruction, Unable to work in a team,' and a few paltry transparent phrases so it didn't look vindictive. He breathed hard but wasn't making much oxygen.

Yolanda said, 'Hello,' to the man who owned the small grocery store on the corner by her house and bought some milk and went up to her flat. She sat down on the chair she had bought from the second-hand shop around the corner and listened to the traffic going by, to the aircraft overhead and to human voices outside on the street. She could see out of her window to the other side of the road, to the other dwellings arranged line after line to the high blocks reaching for the sky, she could see and hear the city night and day.

Yolanda settled down and put her books on the arm of her chair. Apart from a few small clouds, the sky was blue all the way to space, blue that pasted over the nothingness behind it. Somehow the planet moved on, forward, only forward, as if there was no yesterday. It rolled on. Yolanda picked up her first book. It was called *Birth*.

Emma and Sharon sat eating oven chips. They sat on the settee and Sue was in the kitchen. The girls were wary of their mother. She went into the living room, 'Did you have a good play – was it fun on the swing?'

Her voice was a little shaky, the question was forced and unnatural. The two daughters nodded and looked down at the chips on the plate.

'Well Mummy's going to be busy for another half an hour tidying up. It won't take long so you two can go out for a bit longer.'

The girls didn't want to go out. They knew that something was wrong with mum. They wanted to help and cooperate. Emma wanted her dad and wanted to go to school. Sharon was frightened. They didn't want Sue shouting at them anymore. After they finished the chips, Sue gave them each a plastic glass with a carbonated sugary drink in it. When they had finished that she said, 'Go on – you can play out until I've finished tidying this up,' and she gestured to the room and opened the front door for the girls to go back out.

Emma and Sharon walked slowly over to the swing. 'How long is half an hour,' asked Sharon.

Emma said, 'It's not a really long time,' and smiled as

time crawled by.

Natalie saw the girls were back outside the next time she was in her kitchen and muttered under her breath. She wanted to go and play with them, or ask them into her house or take them to the shop with her but Sue's words rang in her head. *I don't want you near my girls*.

Traffic moved down every street of the city. Motorised vehicles found their way down every stretch of terrain and every piece of concrete. A man climbed out of an old car that he had parked on the road that ran along the edge of the estate. He turned back into the vehicle and pulled out a shoulder bag that had the logo of a sporting goods manufacturer on estate. He had on a baseball cap and was wearing sandals. He was in his mid-forties.

Emma and Sharon were both on the swing, standing up and facing one another. Emma was encouraging Sharon to bend her legs and lean back to get the swing moving. Natalie was in the kitchen watching them. Wayne was playing by her feet. The man from the car walked down the ramp into the estate and sat down on the bench that was cut into the wall, twenty feet from the swing. He put down his bag next to him.

The roads that ran through the city ran past hospitals and past prisons and past hospitals for the mentally ill and you could see people going in and see people coming out. The prison brooded over its neighbourhood. Its walls dominated the roads and the barred windows could only be glimpsed from certain angles. In the grey massive gates went men in uniform and special compartmented vans and lorries carrying shackled men in each locked stall. There were times when families went in to see the men inside and times when men who had been inside walked out.

This man had walked out of the prison gates. Now he sat in the afternoon sun and pulled a sandwich from his bag. And he took out a newspaper and spread it on his lap. He went back inside the bag and pulled out a pouch of tobacco – with his hat over his forehead you could not see his eyes. He lit his hand-rolled cigarette. The smoke exhaled was grey and purple and drifted away. He tapped at the cigarette with his forefinger and the ash fell to the ground.

Underneath the city trains ran on tracks through tunnels slowly heating the earth. And trains ran on tracks above the ground and above the roads so that you can see inside someone's bedroom when sitting in a carriage. Buses scuttled around from place to place and youths roamed around on motor scooters. Boats tripped up and down the river and aircraft descended in an always refreshing line towards the biggest airport. It was an endless circulation and you could not guess its purpose.

Sue's two daughters were standing on the swing and it was swinging forward and back and then Sharon sat herself down on the tyre and began to scrape her feet on the floor. The swing slowed down. When it was almost stopped Sharon slipped off and went and leant, half hanging off, against the frame. Emma let the swing slow down until it barely rocked at all.

Natalie filled the kitchen sink with warm water. She went and collected up some plastic bricks from a box in the corner and put Wayne on the draining board in just his nappy and let him splash in the sink with his feet and some plastic bricks to splash happily in the water. From her place by the sink Natalie could see the girls. She couldn't see the man on the bench. He was too far round to the left.

The sun beat down onto the tarmac, onto the concrete

and into the bricks. Heat bounced off the ungiving surfaces and the air was still. Sharon was sitting on the ground leaning back against the frame of the swing. Emma was letting the swing dawdle to a halt. The man on his bench wiped his lips and reached inside his bag.

Natalie could see the girls but she couldn't see the man and she couldn't see the ramp down from the road. The man brought a small hand-held video camera out of the bag and placed it on the bench next to his thigh. The newspaper was placed to lie over it. He put his cigarette in his left hand and snapped open the viewing screen on the camera with his right. He touched a button and the camera whirred quietly, electrically. He could see the screen and he could adjust the zoom lens.

Emma got off the swing and went and sat next to Sharon. Lethargy inhabited the afternoon heat. The girl lay down by her sister. The man on the bench looked down from under his cap to the screen on the camera under the newspaper and pushed in the zoom button. A bus rumbled along to the bus stop and no birds moved at all. The children did not talk and random sounds drifted quietly in the air.

It was hot and still and quiet. Wayne gurgled happily in the sink and Natalie cooled her face with the cold water. Out of sight the man on the bench was sweating and puffing at the very last centimetres of his hand-rolled cigarette. His right hand moved beneath the newspaper, his attention constantly split between his little screen and the view from under the peak of his hat.

Emma looked over towards the bench and saw the man and behind him saw a woman walking down the ramp onto the estate. Sharon saw her sister looking and followed her gaze. There was something familiar about this woman, about her shape. Emma glanced at Sharon and then looked back and the woman was a bit closer. The man on the bench was zooming in on the girls, focusing in on their anatomy.

Emma stood up and when she saw her big sister stand up Sharon stood up and the woman walking towards them was quickening her step and looking at them intently. Then she was near enough to be able to raise an arm and do a half wave and Emma looked at Sharon who looked at Emma and said, 'Aunty Maggie.'

Maggie's face was carrying a wide smile and she greeted them, 'Hello, hello,' while some yards from them and Emma smiled and raised an arm in a shy half wave back. Sharon stepped closer to her sister quite unsure.

'Is mummy in?' Maggie asked with her next step, and Emma managed a nod and Maggie said, 'Well come on let's go and see her,' and now she was at the swing with them and gestured them towards their own front door and put her hand on their backs to usher them home. The girls began to lead the way to Sue's.

Maggie looked over her shoulder. She saw the man on the bench. She said to the two girls, 'Go to mummy's, I'll only be a minute,' and walked over towards the man. She saw him drop his cigarette and start folding his newspaper. She saw the video camera beside his leg on the bench. He began to pick up the camera, to snap shut the viewing screen, to put his finger on the on and off switch. He began to put it in his bag.

Maggie accelerated her walk until every other step was a short run. She didn't want him to get up. He slipped the camera into his bag and looked up and saw her coming.

She dropped her bag on the floor and her raised arm propelled her clubbed fist down on his face as he cowered and her other hand clumped into the back of his head. He got up in a stooped crab-like walk as Maggie's swinging arm wrapped around his neck and a knee thumped into his thigh. He was trying to edge away and walk and scurry and Maggie's breath was panting hard enough to raise and lower all her ribs. Her face was red and sweat popped out but as he took more steps she went after him and swung another fist into his face and swung another fist into his face and kicked hard at his shins but he didn't go down.

Maggie squatted down gasping and he trotted away with his bag – his cap lay on the floor. The sun beat down. She stood up. Sweat dropped down her face. She was shaking all over. Her hand was sore. Her foot was sore. Her heart rate was up and rapid. Maggie opening her mouth and took lungfuls stood hand on hips and then took a few steps back to her bag.

Slowly she put back the things that had spilled out of her bag. Slowly she stood up. She began to walk towards her sister's house and begun to get her breath back. Maggie breathed hard and fought for some composure.

She stopped by the ramp and pulled a tissue from her bag and wiped it across her forehead and around her neck. She walked away slowly and deliberately towards Sue's front door and Natalie from her window smiled and picked up Wayne and said, 'Come on you,' and she carried him into her living room and sat him down beside her and she pulled out a picture book and soon he slept and Natalie dozed and Natalie knew that Emma and Sharon were going to be alright.

The city hosts small and larger squares of green, of grass and trees and pond. The parks fill up when the sun blazed down and the people go to the grass areas and gather in groups and laze around and expose their flesh to the burning rays, filtered through a sky thinned by exhaust gases. There are older people and younger people and parents with children and always men and women exercising their dogs.

Toddlers play on the swings supervised by mothers and nannies and a group of young teenagers gather under a tree. There are three girls and five boys and they are growing into, just beginning, to feel their adult bodies and find out about all that. One girl had walked away from the group with one boy. Another girl is standing up kissing a boy. Her friend stands beside her watching. Three more boys are lying on the grass talking and watching. After a while the girl and the boy stop kissing. The boy walks away turning his back on everyone so they cannot see his kissing. The boy makes a joke to the girl who was watching and then chases her. Another boy stands up and starts kissing the girl.

There is no anxiety or shame as the girl practices her kissing and the boy practices his kissing and their friends laugh lightly and hope they might get a turn and she stands shifting their lips locked and their bodies barely touching. The sun can't reach this shady part but the warmth of the day lets their flesh steam. The other girl is chased back and the kissing stops and they sit together laughing and talking.

Two magpies take off and fly together to a tree and land on separate branches only yards apart. There is enough wind to bend the small boughs on the tree, to bustle through the leaves, to draw up the dust in corners of the concrete spaces and to blow away the blue haze of smoke from the small circle of friends gathered outside the back door of The Cricketers public house.

They finish smoking and go back inside and the music is no longer playing but more drinks are on the table and Paul says, 'I will always think of him as Isaiah.'

And Mick says, 'What's in a name anyway?'

Lucy had a quiet voice and slow measured pace, 'Well, I shall call you Fish,' she said.

And Dan said, 'I know why he was called Isaiah.'

And someone said, 'Why then?'

And Dan said, 'It was because one eye was higher than the other.'

'That's right, that's right,' said Roger.

'I know why he drank all the time,' said Paul, and Lucy and Mick looked at him and he continued, 'He smashed his leg up. He's got a busted thigh. He told me the only time it stopped hurting was after his third drink.'

Around the table different conversations broke out and Lucy said to Dan, 'What was it like at the cemetery?'

Paul told her about the grave with the other boxes and the priest. Lucy sipped her drink and then sipped it again.

'And now here we are and people don't even know his name.'

Staff Nurse Lucerne sat in a small room with soft cushions in it. Lucy had her feet up on a low coffee table and held a mug of tea. Fondant was with her.

'When are you going to give this up?' she asked.

'Oh I don't think I ever will,' said Lucerne, as she rested into the back of the chair and held her hot drink on her chest below her chin.

An ambulance set off across the city streets whooping and wailing through the traffic. On another hospital level Pat Driscombe took grieving parents into her office and downstairs another acre of sheets were cleaned and dried. A doctor injected a man with morphine and took away the pain of the decay into death. Upstairs a child was born and cried its first.

A man stands outside the front of a small terraced house. His arms are folded and his back rests against the blue door. Three large men with shaved heads stand up close to him speaking. Five metres from them two policemen are watching. There is another man with a clipboard and another man with a file of papers. They wear ties.

A large glossy black car pulls up and a man in his twenties gets out and lights a cigarette. He talks to the men wearing ties. In an agitated and impatient manner, he walks over to the house inhaling smoke. Nothing really happens for some time. It's an eviction, a repossession of property.

Then the man with his back to the door looks like he might cry. His face softens and the tension leaves his lower hip which droops a bit. He turns around and taking a key from his pocket opens the door. Immediately the first man with a shaved head is past him and inside.

Another one of the three is talking sympathetically to the man who was holding out against the bailiffs. He is allowed to go back inside and he brings out two children's bicycles. The house looks empty. He wants to shake hands with the young man from the glossy black car. He wants a bit of dignity in defeat. The landlord manages it before turning away indifferent and counting the cost.

Lucerne says to Fondant, 'Come on,' and the two women walk back onto the ward.

In The Cricketers a few more people have joined the table where John's friends have gathered. The volume of talk has risen as more alcohol has been consumed. Music is playing continuously.

Paul is talking to Lucy. He is animated and flushed red with the booze. He says, 'I know why you didn't come. I know why.'

Lucy is used to Paul, used to his company and to seeing him enthused with drink. 'Why? Why then? – tell me.'

Paul sat back and looked at her, 'You were scared.'

'What?' said Lucy.

'Yeah, you were scared. You really liked him and you were scared to see what it was like.'

'What, what was it like?' Lucy was a little challenging but comfortable with the way Paul got agitated when he wanted to express something.

'You were scared to see what it was like to see him in there with no fucker giving a fuck and nothing...'

Lucy looked at Paul, and she saw the upset in his face and the tears starting from his eyes and Paul looked at Lucy and before she looked away he saw the fixed line of her mouth and a drop of wetness almost spilling from her eyes. He rocked his head back and looked at the ceiling and felt a closing of his throat. He wanted to groan but didn't.

Lucy stood up in her black-laced heeled shoes and walked in her leather jacket to the door marked Ladies. Inside she dabbed at her eyes with tissues to stop the thick mascara running onto the china-white foundation. She plumped up her black hair.

Paul was at the bar. He pulled a note out of his pocket. It was all the money he had. He bought a drink for Lucy and Mick and one for himself. They were John's friends.

Sometimes the wind blew from the south and the humid air would drop rain and the rain carried yellow particles of sand from the desert. Cars parked in city streets accrued a little yellow dust from the far south and air was close and sweaty.

Dr Jones was feeling a little uncertainty in his gastric tract and a distant clamping feeling in his shoulders and neck. At one time he felt a sort of shocking pain in his arm, but then it was gone. He looked around at the other people having lunch. He noted their wealth, the rings sporting diamond clusters and the expensive shoes and fine jackets. His cash balance in his current account was greater than the price of an average house.

Some people on the city streets had the pallor of heat exhaustion but Dr Jones was fresh and maintained in air-conditioned buildings and vehicles. He was eating a smoked salmon salad with dark crunchy bread. The girls serving him were from Sweden and Slovakia. He always asked.

He had considered writing to the Director of Clinical Services regarding Yolanda's psychiatric assessment and perhaps suggesting a review – as any concerned parent would. And he considered suggesting some private treatment and then he had decided it was all fine as it was. After all she had emergency psychiatric assessment at the nearest possible accident and emergency location so perhaps one had to accept she was, sadly, someone with serious mental health issues. It was terribly sad but even growing up Gwen and he had noticed things about her.

The humidity grew with a storm intensity during the afternoon until lightning flickered and thunder made its first rumble from the darker grey of a grew sky. Jones was back in the office and was trying to loosen a discomforting stiffness in his shoulders. It didn't matter what she said, she was mad. And the other thing was he hated his name. Always had. The ordinariness of it was repulsive. Like those makes of cars that everyone had. No, he wanted another name. Funny he had always like Jeremy.

The lightning ripped through the grey sky. Electric white fluttering for a moment and then gone and then the pause and the magnificent low grumble rolling around the low heavens. People looked up at the sky, at the clouds and the rain started and the air cooled and then more lightning, and rumbles capped with explosive bursts.

Yolanda opened all the windows in her home and let in the storm breeze and watched the electric currents fly through the sky and smiled a greeting of appreciation for every roaring decibel of thunder. The rain poured down and danced on the pavements and made streams of the gutters. In moments everything was washed down and refreshed.

She sat down and began to look at her books about birth and began to learn all there was to see and to know. There was the physiology and the cultural and the historical and the political and scientific and all that everything. And from everything she was learning she made a plan. Yolanda could see a way that kept away her greatest fear, the most terrible dread.

You could see the dread everywhere. The stainless steel and the scalpels for cutting. The bright lights and the child held up screaming like some trophy. People gathered around. Doctors in gowns and masks. Doctors like him. Like he was controlling them and he could even be there. An understanding of the moment of openness, of vulnerability.

The storm went away. A gentle breeze swept through the trees. The air was calm.

Yolanda went to her corridor and looked out. The city was there rolling away to the river and up the other side to far off heaths distant in the haze. In this mass was everything Yolanda needed, every idea and means to allow her to open herself.

The sun sweltered on and inside her cells divided and grew and Yolanda let every moment grow into her mind, into her thoughts. Night would come and she could lie there and see that this movement and this development were going forward like a thousand generations before. Now there was to be a final change. A beginning and an end.

Richard Jones looked out of the window over the garden towards the pool. He walked into the room where Gwen was watching television and walked out again. He was waiting for Adrian to come over. He was going to talk to Adrian about his sister. Adrian would have to make more time for her now. He would have to visit more often to make sure she was doing OK. He could take Sarah, his new girlfriend over. Richard Jones wanted to keep in touch, involved and close.

The moon glared down. Night was still warm and the city revved its endless engine through Yolanda's windows. She looked down at her strong body, her tanned skin and began to note when changes would begin. When would the swollen womb nudge up above the pubic bone and when, week by week, would this happen. Or even now how big is this thing growing inside her. How big today and how big tomorrow and how big in ten weeks and how big at forty weeks. Everything was changing and every day was bringing the new life closer.

Adrian spoke with his father about visiting Yolanda more often. He could see it could be useful. Richard Jones couldn't quite understand why Adrian didn't seem so keen on getting Sarah involved. He saw a shadow of discomfort on his son's face when he suggested that she might get friendly with Yolanda.

'Anyway, I ordered the new CX5 for you,' said Jones, 'It's the one with the two-litre diesel.'

'Oh excellent – I saw the figures for its urban cycle,' said Adrian and he and his father spoke about comparative car specifications for twenty-five minutes.

Yolanda looked at the room with the window. She looked at the soft blue carpet and the plain white walls. It was up half a flight of stairs from the bathroom. It was comfortable and clean. There was a lot of space and just one chair. If visitors came there was a mattress. It was light and you could see clouds, the moon, the sky. This was her home. This is where it would happen.

Maggie sat on the settee in Sue's house. Emma sat beside her on one side and Sharon on the other. Sue was holding the vacuum cleaner. She had turned it off. Maggie was still mopping sweat off her face and neck. 'I was just catching up on this,' said Sue meaning the cleaning of the house.

'Oh I know,' said Maggie, 'Take your eye off it for a day and next thing you know it's chaos.'

Sharon and Emma were looking at their aunt. They had not seen her for a very long time. Maggie was struggling to keep her composure. Her younger sister had long ago decided Maggie's laid-back easy-going ways did not match her ambition or standards. Now all Maggie could see was Sue's house had been trashed and the kids were being kept off school and left playing out in the estate.

Maggie's hand hurt. Sharon looked at it and said, 'What have you done?'

'I fell over and dropped my handbag.'

'Do you want something for it?' asked Sue.

'I'll run it under the tap,' said Maggie, and going into the kitchen she saw two bottles of alcohol, the ashtrays and dirty dishes and the complete collapse of Sue's smart domestic veneer. There was no towel or cloth to dry her hand on so she shook it and went into the other room. Sue was collecting up three newspapers that had sprawled onto the floor.

'Oh leave that now,' said Maggie and went on, 'I haven't seen you or your lovely daughters for ages – let's have a chat.'

Sue stopped and said, 'Cup of tea or glass of wine?'

'Tea,' said Maggie.

The girls relaxed and Sue went to put on the kettle.

Maggie spent a few minutes talking to Sharon and Emma. She asked the names of their teachers and who their best friend was. She said they looked very grown up and that their hair was lovely.

Sue stood by the back door smoking. Maggie said to the two girls, 'Come on show me your room,' and went upstairs with them. Sue finished her cigarette and Maggie came downstairs.

'I've got them doing a tidy up,' she said.

The two women sat in silence for a minute. You could hear an aircraft crossing the sky and the coming and going drone of cars. Sometimes you hear the leaves rustling in the tree by the corner of the block. There was a thud and door slamming. It sounded close. Probably next door. Sue winced.

Maggie went over to the back door and looked out into the yard. It was a sun trap. She took a couple of steps outside and looked back at Sue's home. From where she was, she could see the upstairs windows of the houses to the left and right. The sound of a child crying out across the fences. Maggie went back inside.

'Has Will left you?' she asked.

'No, he's away working,'

'Been gone long?'

'A few days.'

Sue looked away her eyes overloaded with tears. Maggie said, 'Emma and Sharon are fine. You're a great mum. They'll be fine.'

Sue's throat filled with hurt. A great glot of something was in her neck as if she wanted to cry out, as if crying out was the only way to clear it. She felt the taste of vomit at the top of her nose. A tear spilled down her face.

Sue opened her mouth to speak but gagged on a sob. She sat on the settee and twisted both her elbows into the armrest and her back shook one big wrench, she choked on an intake of air, the sour taste in her nose came through and tears ran from her eyes. She shook again. Then her open mouth gasped and gasped. Her face screwed up and dribble ran out of her mouth. A low groan came from her.

Maggie sat beside her. She put a hand in the small curve of her back. Sue gasped in air and groaned and then began to ride out the sobs that shook her. The tears flowed off her face onto her arms. A string of saliva hung off her teeth and her jaws opened a little and then shut with each intake of breath. She quietened a bit. Maggie said nothing.

Sue gasped and sobbed and groaned again and then sat up from her place on the corner of the settee and another low groan and more sobs and she said, 'It was me, Maggie. It was me, Maggie. It wasn't anyone else. It was me.'

Sue stood up and walked across the room. She walked into her kitchen. Her shoulders shuddered a little and her breath was unsteady. She pulled some dishes and cups and glasses out of the sink and ran the tap. The water was cold on her face. She splashed it onto her neck and let some run down her back and between her breasts.

She filled her hands with cold water and splashed it on her forehead and onto her hair. She spread it all over the back of her neck and let it run down her spine. Her breath came deep and strong and straight.

Then there was a shudder through her and another breath and she ran the tap for a bit over her hands. Another tear spilt over her eyelash and she said, 'Now,' and her voice was loose around the edges but firm. She walked next door and her daughters sat on the settee with her sister. She sat beside them and said, 'I'm alright now.'

School was out and children came home onto the estate and mothers stood and talked behind pushchairs. You could hear small feet running between the blocks, and shouted instructions, 'Come here,' 'Stop it.'

Ben was walking over to Dan's place to pick up a quarter-ounce of black of hash and Alan was down at the snooker club trying to sell a credit pushchair. The teacher had found the day less distressing without the presence of the little girl stirring up worry and concern.

Sharon was sitting on Maggie's lap. Maggie stroked her niece's hair when it fell down from the back of her head. Maggie asked, 'Sue, have you got any money?'

'Will left me loads to get me through OK.'

'Two hundred?' asked Maggie.

'And the rest…' said Sue.

'I've an idea,' said Maggie.

There were some elevated roads across the city. Roads that flew above the housing and the shops, that were laid on giant trestles. Other roads were urban freeways where cars and commercial vehicles flew through neighbourhoods, three lanes across. In other places you found roads sweeping through wastelands or between wastelands. Suddenly the vehicles found space and freedom to make speed on roads laid between factories and housing blocks.

A road like this curved from the edge of a place where tower blocks of housing rose up and flew south through a desolate landscape of rundown factories and unkempt open spaces until up rose the mighty clean towers of commerce. Great blocks rose more than twenty-five-storeys high placed beside the river where ships once landed cargo. One block of steel and glass had red writing on its top edge and another had blue letters. A third was anonymous and there were other smaller less significant new modern constructions scattered around, but nothing was older than twenty years.

Thousands of people went into these office blocks and operated the administrations of credit systems. Some were paid ordinary sums and some were paid extraordinary amounts. Here there were people who had two houses, yachts and fast new cars. Early in the morning and late at night buses dropped off the people who cleaned the corridors and rooms.

During the day the workforce had a similar look. Men wore matching trousers and jackets and tied a piece of cloth around their neck. The women wore skirts and dresses and sometimes trousers and all presented their hair and hands in a certain way and all the fabrics they wore were looking new. People all moved towards the buildings at the same time in the morning and moved away from them at the same time in the evening.

Their obedience was rewarded with scales of pay and pensions and progression. There were young men who fought at market coal faces who were coated in cash. And there were men who operated all this, and managed all this, who had more money than they could count.

It was two miles from the blocks massing against the sky to The Cricketers where now John's friends were mostly inebriated, drunk and laughing. Amy arrived and ordered a large beer. She went and sat with Lucy and asked, 'Did you go?' and Lucy told her, 'No,' and gave her the description of the scene that Paul had drawn for her. Amy drank her beer. Lucy sipped at her drink. Amy looked around at the gathering now swollen to more than twenty people and said, 'Not a bad turn out though,' and Lucy agreed 'Especially as no one knew what had happened to him.'

Mick slipped into the seat next to Amy.

'How's your nurse?' she asked him.

He winces.

Amy speculates, 'Nothing doing?'

Mick twirls his beer glass between his finger and thumb and smiles with a grimace. He is wearing a clean and ironed shirt. His hair is neatly cut and his jeans freshly washed. He looks at Amy and looks away.

'I can't really explain it,' he says.

'Well go on try then,' says Amy lightly.

Mick is grateful to her for her wanting to know. 'It's difficult to explain. I think it's something to do with the job.'

Amy pushed her long red hair behind her ear. She could see a cloud across Mick's face. She said, 'What the hours and stuff?'

'No not that.'

'Glamourous highly paid doctors.'

Mick grinned easily. 'No, it's nothing like that.'

He sat forward looking at the table, drinking, seeing if Amy's attention would hold.

She leant forward and said, 'Come on. Spill, what do you mean?'

People were talking about Isaiah, about John, about the evenings they had spent with him. They were swapping anecdotes and recalling adventures and mishaps and scrapes. He was being remembered for his good heartedness and his stupidity.

Mick glanced up at Amy. 'I think if you do that job properly it drains you, you know, if you care.'

Amy nodded. He went on, 'She's fantastic at it. Gives out love all day.'

Mick sipped at his beer and looked away. Amy could see him in profile and saw his throat jump as he swallowed hard.

Paul walked over to the table and looked down at Mick and Amy. He looked at Lucy. Roger came and stood beside him.

Paul was swaying a bit. He leant forward. 'It's not fucking right,' he said. Roger nodded in agreement.

'No,' said Lucy, 'Not much is, is it?'

'No, it's all fucking wrong.'

Mick looked up at Paul. His face was flamed red with the alcohol. His glasses were held together by a piece of tape. Paul wore ill-fitting second-hand clothes. He was upset and hurting. Mick said, 'What is it?'

Paul said, 'It's all fucking wrong. Slung in the ground like that. No headstone. Nothing.'

Mick, Lucy, Amy, and Roger looked at him, and looked away. Paul stood up and brought his beer glass up to his mouth. He took large mouthfuls. Some beer spilt down out of the side of his mouth.

Lucy said, 'You could do something about it.'

The jukebox was playing a rebel song about prisoners being shipped abroad for stealing the corn to feed their children and out on the street a police car zapped past with just its blue light flashing. An old lady pushed her shopping in front of her on a wheeled trolley and a man carried his crippled son on his back. Clouds were filling the sky, cutting across the sun. The air stayed warm and humid.

Staff Nurse Lucerne walked out of the hospital and stood at the bus stop waiting. Her back was aching again. The bus came and she went home.

Every revolution of the planet they call a day and day passes and night passes day and now all that has gone has gone forever. This passing is time and in time everything changes and skin is creased and bones are aged and seasons come and go as the planet draws away from the star that gives it heat. And then spins through space for weeks and months and then comes back close to give another summer.

There was a time when airplanes fought death fights above the city streets. There were times when high explosives ripped down the city streets. No longer do you see young men die, bleed and burn, up against this blue sky. No longer do they have to do that war.

You can count the time in years or months or weeks or minutes but you cannot shift it back a single millimetre. Now all the people carry little black boxes into which they speak. Now children sit manipulating electronic images with their thumbs. People cannot speak to strangers, only to the black boxes they carry in their hands.

Yolanda grew her child in her fit and healthy body and watched and felt every change. Now you are going forward and cannot go back, now the next season of humanity is on its way. Her womb expanded and grew above her pubic bone and grew and filled with fluid around the child and with every moment, every minute, every day, the birth was coming. Change was every day and everything was changing.

In the beginning you were counting months and then weeks and then living every day in a hiatus of wait. Every moment of it not happening, a moment nearer the moment when it will start, when it will begin, when Yolanda becomes something else. Something sacred. The moon is in the sky and she sits in her home and holds her full belly and waits. Waits for time.

The days have lengthened until you reach the longest day and then they shorten and summer fades and Yolanda wakes with unease and walks through the shops and the market. There is the cramping pain. If it is not starting now, it must start soon. It must. Something has to change. Nothing can stay like this.

Any more cramping pains and back to her home and this should be the beginning but false alarms are common. Yolanda knows the name for the false alarm cramps and she knows the opening to her womb should be dilating as her body releases a chemical. The cramps of the womb beginning to open and she lies in a warm bath and the sun drops down over the city. The light is gone and the bath is warm and the cramps are intensifying. This is not an alarm.

Then out of the bath and up into her room and lying down. Suddenly out floods warm fluid. She calls the midwife. Now the baby is coming. Now the baby is coming down. Now the baby is going to be born.

You can feel him coming and surging and going and coming. Inside the baby is dropping down the canal, down between your bones head first. Here comes the next life. Hormones loosen the joints, loosen the pelvic link and down comes the baby.

The midwife is happy. She can see it's going well. Yolanda stands up and the next surge lets down the baby and the next lets it down again.

She puts a mirror on the floor and with the next crescendo the midwife says, 'You can see the head,' and now the baby is crowning, now Yolanda stands and it's almost here almost…

One more and it comes and it overwhelms and Yolanda breathes and the midwife is holding the head and another rush and there is another voice, from the heavens, from all the miracles that there have ever been, from every act of faith there comes another voice. In the room you hear a cry. A child is here. A cry.

Someone else's cry. Someone else has spoken. On Yolanda's belly below between her breasts lies another person. Yolanda is a mother. Yolanda has a daughter. The girl child splutters a little. She is wrapped in a blanket. The moon shines through the window. The midwife is cleaning up. The planet is rotating through space.

You cannot go back.

There is another person.

Now Yolanda knows love.

The sand comes up between Sue's toes. It squeezes through the gaps and spreads a bit. A film of sea washes over her feet. The sun is on her shoulders and her skin is brown. Her feet look fine and evenly tanned and strong. The water runs around them and washes away the sand. She takes another step.

Sharon and Emma are thirty yards further out to sea. The beach shelves so gently the water is barely above their knees. They jump when little waves come pounding in. Maggie walks up to Sue, comes alongside her.

'You're not going back, are you?'

'No. I'm not,' says Sue.

The tide is nearly all the way out. The sands are extended by the low water, saturated and flat and wide between chalk headlands. Across the beach men, women and children lie in the sun, sit up, walk to the water and paddle and swim. Some play with bats and balls and some small boys construct a strong point against invasion, with a moat and defensive walls. It is built of sand and less than a foot high.

From the water's edge you could look back over the sands to the resort, white buildings at the seafront then climbing back in rows up the hillside. Behind the resort the green downland emerges up and then there is the sky, blue and over there white clouds. There are cries and shouts from children and a dog barks briefly and from overhead the harsh calls of big gulls wheeling away above it all.

'Not at all?' asked Maggie.

'No,' Sue says firmly, and waits a moment and then almost laughing, 'No. I can make it work here.'

'Will?' Maggie was asking not arguing.

'He'll be fine. I don't think where we were was any good for him. And...'

Sue walked on through the sand and water and Maggie walked on with her and nothing more was going to be said.

A man ran past them splashing into the water. He kept running until the water was at his knees and kept on running out until it was at his thighs and he began to slow and then let out a loud exclamation and threw himself forward into the sea and was gone underwater until his head rose up and he stroked away swimming. A man and a woman held a toddler between them, one hand each, and helped her walk through the water and pulled her up when a little wave came in.

'You've got it all planned then?' Maggie asked.

'As much as anything can be,' said Sue. 'Everything is uncertain really. But if the kids are in school down here, I can make everything else work.'

'It's a big change.'

'Yeah, great isn't it,' said Sue, affecting a confidence that showed an edge of doubt.

'I'll be down all the time,' said Maggie.

'Sure,' said Sue, and the city seemed further away than just miles and its mass insignificant behind the soft greens of field and woodland and acres of wheat growing more golden under rays and beams of light. Now all the hedges were overflowing onto the lanes and byways, were all heavy with broad leaves and flowers were all over pasture and garden.

On the beach human beings walked and ran and edged out into the water to swim. The sun was on their flesh and limbs were stretched out and some let their minds go and dozed. A breeze ruffled through the down on skin and through the hair on arms and chests and hair lay matted with sea water.

Out between the headland the sea turned blue reflecting the sky, the sea that had born a generation of young men away to die on other beaches fighting evil. An aircraft tore a white vapour trail from the sky, innocuous now with only leisure travellers on board.

'It can't be like this in winter,' said Maggie.

Sue laughed and looked up at the sun and felt its heat on her face and the salt and sea had faded her hair blonde and brought out brown freckles on her nose and across her cheeks. Her teeth were white in her tanned face.

'I know that,' and the sun dipped into a cloud and it was immediately cooler and Sue continued, 'But,' and she looked at her sister with a playful lightness around her mouth, 'I know the ways of the world,' and watched Maggie's face getting a questioning tone before finishing, 'Then it will be summer again, won't it?'

Acknowledgements

Thank you to all those who have held me close.

Ray Leigh was born in London and raised in Essex before returning to the great city on the Thames.

He published *CLEAR* in 2020 – a novella, or prose poem, or maybe just poetry. Its fluid form telling stories of cops and crime in a cinematic drama.

Revolutions continues the challenge to the literary orthodoxy with a novel of unafraid intensity.

Leigh's work confronts and disturbs with a perspective drawn from a tough emotional landscape where, always, love wins all.

He lives and works in London.

BAD PRESS iNK

publishers of niche, alternative and cult fiction

Visit

www.BADPRESS.iNK

for details of all our books, and sign up to
be notified of future releases and offers

Also from BAD PRESS iNK

'On a clear day you can see forever'

London's seedy underbelly ripped apart by razor sharp distilled prose

CLEAR by Ray Leigh

How well do we really know the ones we love?

Especially once they are dead?

My Husband's Child by Allison Lee

Welcome to The King George.

You know it. Your old local. Back in the day.

The stink of beer and piss, sticky carpets, nicotine stains on the ceiling, soggy bar towels, and the chance of a punch-up on a Saturday night – or anytime for that matter.

And in amongst it all an awkward 20-year-old, trapped behind the bar, with nothing to do but pull pints and wait for the next fag break.

Until he finds Amy. And life. And an escape – if he dares.

The Sadness of The King George by Shaun Hand

Get Carter meets *Sons of Anarchy* in this gritty British crime thriller series.

From being in a gang to becoming a gangster, the Heavy Duty trilogy invented Biker Noir.

Damage's club has had an offer it can't refuse, to patch over to join The Brethren MC. But as the bikes rumble and roar across the wild Northern fells, what does this mean for Damage and his brothers? What choices will they have to make as they ride through the wind? What bloody oil-stained history might it reawaken? And why are The Brethren making this offer? Loyalty to his club and his brothers has been Damage's life and route to wealth, but what happens when business becomes serious and brother starts killing brother?

The Heavy Duty trilogy by Iain Parke

Important Notice – Please Read

BAD PRESS iNK Limited as the publisher of this book does not give permission for it to be used for the training of Large Language Models, Artificial Intelligence or any similar systems other than by prior written agreement of the publisher, or on the contractual terms below.

Default training usage contract

By obtaining and using the contents of this book for the training of Large Language Models, Artificial Intelligence or any similar systems without the prior written agreement of BAD PRESS iNK Limited (the 'Publisher') you (the 'User') are deemed to accept these contractual terms and agree to pay the publisher a licence fee of £10,000.

This fee is deemed due and payable on the date the User acquires the book text.

The publisher gives notice of our right to add interest and collection costs for late payment under The Late Payment of Commercial Debts (Interest) Act 1998 Act as amended and supplemented by The Late Payment of Commercial Debts Regulations 2002 and Statutory interest will be charged at a rate of 8% over the Bank of England base rate.

The User agrees that the use of this book for the above training purposes is at the User's risk and the publisher offers no warranties and accepts no liability to the User for the use of the text of this book for the above purposes or any consequential losses that may arise.

This contract is governed by and to be construed in accordance with English law and the parties irrevocably submit to the non-exclusive jurisdiction of the Courts of England and Wales in respect of any claim, dispute or difference arising out of or in connection with this contract.

www.ingramcontent.com/pod-product-compliance
Lightning Source LLC
Chambersburg PA
CBHW061119100726
47911CB00013B/608